Nicholas E V

Murder

Lost in Time

Nicholas E Watkins

The Eastbourne Murders

Book 2

A Mandy Pile

Mystery

About the Author

Nicholas Watkins lives on the South Coast and is the Author of the Tim Burr series of spy novels. He has four children. He worked as an accountant for many years in the City of London.

Murder Lost in Time

Copyright © Nicholas E Watkins 2020

.

Chapter 1

"I am getting too old for this," groaned Carlos Alto as he pressed the alarm clock button. It was five thirty and still dark outside. Next to him his wife groaned and pulled the duvet off him, as she rolled over in the bed trying to ignore his moaning and groaning. She was soon back to sleep. Carlos sat on the side of the bed and lit a cigarette. He had a good cough and made his way to the bathroom.

It was October and it was blowing a small gale and raining heavily by the time Carlos drove along the Eastbourne seafront. It was a high tide and the waves were crashing against the pebble beach. There was a surprising amount of traffic at this early hour for a sleepy seaside town. It was mini rush hour for the mechanics, builders and transport workers. The next rush would be in about an hour and a half when the school run would clog the streets.

By the time he pulled up at the block of flats just a road back from the pier, it was half past six. The building was shrouded in scaffolding. The plasterers, who were scheduled to render the outside of the block of flats, sat around in their vans, eating their breakfast and drinking tea waiting for the rain to stop.

Carlos pulled his coat collar up and braced himself for the onslaught of the wind and rain as he stepped from the cab of his Transit Van. He passed the painted sign on its side, "Alto Plumbing' as he made his way to the rear and pulled out the bag containing his tools.

"I am definitely getting to old for this," he repeated as he pushed his way against the chilling wind and made his way into the building.

"Flat six," said the foreman hardly acknowledging Carlos. "and get it done quickly we are running weeks behind schedule."

"It's not my fault.." began Carlos but was waived away as another tradesman approached the foreman for instructions.

He made his way up the rubble and dust covered stairs to the third floor and went into the flat. "Morning," said Tom. Tom was Carlo's plumbers mate and apprentice. A lad in his late teens, he was surprising keen and kept good time. In contrast Carlos was approaching sixty two, sick and tired of getting up early, getting covered in dirt and felt he had seen enough copper pipe to last a life time.

"Morning, okay let's make a start," said Carlos. He rummaged in his bag and pulled out the specification for the flat he was in. "Right, bathroom, shower," he looked round the the flat getting his bearings and comparing the reality to the drawing he held in his hand.

The interior walls had been studded out. The joiners had created the walls using lengths of timber to create the frame and nailed plaster boards to form the internal walls. After the electrical wiring and any water pipes had been installed the plasterers would come in and skim the walls.

The area where the en suite toilet and shower were to be housed were part of the existing structure and as such had not been touched. Carlos studied the plans one more time as he surveyed the existing layout. The bath and toilet had been ripped out but little else. "Looks like we will have to hack the tiles off and knock a few holes in the wall to put the pipe work in," said Tom.

Tom being young, Carlos knew that he loved nothing better than knocking things down, "Get the sledge hammer out of the van and then you can work up a bit of a sweat." He handed Tom the keys and waited for his return.

When lunch time arrived the flat looked considerable worse for wear than when Carlos and Tom had turned up that morning. "We have the plumbing in for the toilet, bath and sink, not bad going so far. We should be able to get away a bit early with a bit of luck. The shower will be easy. Just knock a small hole in that stud wall. Shove the pipes in. Stick the risers on and connect the tray to the waste and Bob's your Uncle," said Carlos.

"Cup of tea and a fry up in the Cafe on the front?" said Tom.

"You are leaning my boy," said Carlos as they made their way out of the flat for lunch."We'll make a proper plumber of you yet."

It was half past twelve when they made their way back to the bathroom. Carlos pulled a felt tip marker pen from his overalls and began to draw on the wall. "Look we can keep the work to a minim. This is just studding with plaster board. Use the Stanley knife and cut where I have marked then pull the board of with the jemmy."

Tom set to work. "The plaster is really thick."

"Carlos came over. "That is a pretty amateur job. It looks like someone has filled great hole with card board, newspaper and then slapped plaster on it. Never mind just give it bash with the hammer and get it sorted."

Carlos sat back down on the tool box and returned to reading the newspaper. Tom continued to bash at the wall while moaning at the shoddy workmanship. Finally the hammering stopped. "Jesus," Carlos heard Tom say. "The gap behind if full of old plaster. Carlos, they seemed to have poured the left over plaster into the gap before they sealed the hole."

Carlos put the paper down and wandered onto the bathroom. "Yep you're right. That is a lot of muck. We'll have to clean it out before we can run the pipework through there. Go and find a wheel barrow and a shovel." He returned to reading his paper while Tom went in search.

"We getting off early seems to have gone out of the window," said Carlos as Tom returned after nearly an hour with the requisite wheel barrow. "Come on I'll give you a hand to get the crap out from behind the wall."

They began to shovel the semi-dried plaster dust into the barrow. Gradually the gap between the external wall and the stud wall began to empty. "Nearly there," said Tom.

Tom suddenly stopped shovelling. "What's up?" said Carlos.

"There's a black bin sack. Can't you see it?"

He reached and pulled it out. Laying it on the floor, he pushed the plaster dust from the surface and opened it. There was more plaster in side. "Tip it up into the barrow."

He ripped the bag further and up ended it, spilling its contents into the wheel barrow.

"It's a dead cat?" said Tom.

Carlos lent forward and examined the partially mummified object sitting in the pile of dust and rubble. He stepped back letting out a load gasp.

"Oh my God, oh my God," his voice was trembling. "Phone the Police," he gasped.

Chapter 2

She stood in the doorway and pulled her collar up against the cold night air. It was approaching one thirty in the morning and the punters were thin on the ground. She was becoming desperate. She needed money for her fix and she needed to score soon.

She knew there would be more action nearer the clubs and the red-light district. There the girls sat in windows offering their services to the passing customers. They were the lucky ones, warm and protected. They were the acceptable face of prostitution in Amsterdam. She existed on the margins. She rarely made her way to the red-light area. It was dangerous.

She walked over the narrow cobblestone bridge and along the side of the Canal. She was encroaching on rivals territory. Here the girls, mostly Eastern European were protected by their pimps. The protection they offered was from the girl's clients not themselves. They treated the girls like a commodity to be bought and sold, exploiting them to the full. Most were trafficked and worked under threat not only to themselves but also to their families back home.

Being so cold even here there were few punters on the streets. Every possible customer was accosted as the made their way along the street, The girls stepped forward and displayed their wares. Like her they wore very little under their coats. She only had on her bra and knickers.

She felt the need for her fix. She needed money soon. Stepping into the shadows, she removed her underwear and now naked put her coat back on. She heard voices approaching and readied to move into their path and display what she had to offer.

She opened her coat fully revealing her breasts and pubic region. Although desperate she had still had enough of her wits about her to focus on the approaching voices. Something triggered a warning in her brain and she hesitated. She understood. They were speaking in Albanian.

She darted back into the shadows and pulled her coat around her. "Jesus," she said under her breath. "That was close." She watched as the two pimps made their way along the embankment checking their girls and taking the money from them as the went. The Albanians were well known to her and all the other working girls. They were brutal and feared. They showed no kindness or sympathy. To them the girls were no more than a source of income and they showed more empathy to their dogs, which was very little more than they did to the girls they controlled.

She watched as they disappeared from view. She took a deep breath and waited. Finally she was rewarded. He was drunk and stoned, no older than she, in his early twenties. He was English and had come to Amsterdam on a stag weekend. He had lost his friends and had little idea where he was. They had spent the day smoking pot in the various cafes and the night in the strip clubs drinking. He had actually approached her asking directions to his hotel.

He had forgotten his need to get to his hotel bed when she had laid out what was on offer by opening her coat and standing hands on hips showing her naked body.

"How much?" he had asked in a slurred voice as he rocked back and forth unsteady on his feet.

"Two hundred," she had put forward speculatively.

He fumbled through his pockets looking for his money. Eventually he found a pile of crumpled notes and coins in his jeans pockets. He unfolded them and began to count. "I've got forty three euros," he declared proudly after several attempts.

"Cash point on the corner," she suggested.

Slurring, he laughed. "Overdraft, tapped out," he replied.

She believed him. He dressed like a student and she was desperate. "Okay forty three euros, follow me."

She was really jangling by the time he left her flat. She had struggled to get him to climax. She usually avoided drunks if she had a choice. They took too long and often became angry or violent blaming her for their lack of performance. She hurriedly pulled on some clothes and used her phone to text her dealer. She made her way out of the flat onto the street.

She was back in less than ten minutes. Drug delivery was more efficient than home shopping and could easily match any retailer on the internet. She opened her drawer and pulled out her syringes and paraphernalia. She knew the dealer and knew the gear would be good. She felt the excitement build as she draw the liquid into the syringe, through the make shift cotton wool filter from the spoon.

The feeling of well being spread over her and she slipped into a state of semi consciousness. She sat unmoving as the night passed and morning's light arrived in the small grubby flat. She roused herself and readied herself for another day of survival.

She washed and found there was milk and cereal. She ate and sitting on the bed turned on the television. She had learnt to speak Dutch. She realised that she must be one of the few English people to do so. She laughed that she might have a career change as a translator. Hardly a realistic option as most of the Dutch population spoke better English than she.

The BBC news came on and she watched as she ate cornflakes. She recognised Eastbourne Pier and gave the news reader her full attention. The camera focussed on a block of flats clad in scaffolding. News crews were gathered in the road and the police were making a statement.

A young police woman was stood on the pavement answering questions being fired at her from all directions. They were all vying to attract her attention and get their questions answered.

"Inspector Pile, Inspector Pile can you give us further details?" the BBC correspondent was demanding as he thrust the microphone into DCI Mandy Pile's face.

"I have nothing to say at this stage. We are just beginning our investigations and I shall release a statement when we have something to report." She turned her back on the gathered reporters and walked off.

The spoon slipped from her hand and she did not notice as the contents of the bowl spilt onto the bed, She sat stunned staring at the screen now showing the sports news.

"Oh my God, oh my God," she wept as she sat unmoving.

Chapter 3

DCI Mandy Pile struggled to find anywhere to park. The area surrounding the block of flats was packed with news vans, police cars, reporters, TV crews and nosey passers-bye. She had been in Brighton Police Station when the call came in that a body had been found in Eastbourne. The drive to the Seafront had been torturous. The wind was gusting, the rain fell in sheets and the traffic crawled along the A27 from Brighton to Eastbourne. A half an hour journey had taken nearly a hour and a half and she still was not parked up yet.

She gave up looking for a space close to the scene and parked in a loading bay outside the Pier Hotel on the front. She was soaking wet and wind swept by the time she reached the crime scene. "About time," grumbled Detective Sergeant Sam Shaw.

"Nice to see you too," she replied.

"I am wet, cold and fed up of being harassed by this mob." He was referring to the pack of reporters and journalist being held back by the uniformed officers attending.

"Have you been in?"

"No not yet. It was chaos when I got here. Uniform had been called in the first instance, but some dick head, one of the blokes who found the body, decided to post it on Facebook or whatever and this mob appeared. It was more like a football match with the crowd than a crime scene."

"I was just about to go off duty when the call came in."

"I sort of guessed that, the high heels and cocktail dress gave it away. Invite to the Palace was it?" Sam never missed an opportunity to let Mandy know what he thought about posh people.

"I had just changed. It was just a diner at the Savoy with some old chums, actually."

"Well it looks like fish and chips here instead now," he smiled as they made their way past the copper on the door and began to climb the stairs to the flat where the body had been found. "Hard hat," he said passing her one and placing one on his head.

She pushed it on her wet hair. "That completes the drowned rat look I was aiming for," she said.

They reached the entrance. "Who are they?" She indicated the two workmen standing with a police sergeant taking notes.

"Carlos Alto and his mate Tom Porter, they found the remains."

Forensics where already there waiting in living room, dressed in their white coveralls. She nodded in acknowledgement. She and Sam were handed latex gloves and slip over shoe protectors. "Where is it?" She said removing her high heels to cover her feet.

"Bathroom through there," she went in the direction indicated. It was clear that the plumbers were half way through the installation and she could see immediately where the discover had been made. There was a hole in the stud wall where the shower was to go.

"That's a lot of dust, rubble and mess," said Sam. "They will have a job and a half sifting through this lot for evidence."

"Has the scene been recorded?" Mandy replied. She received an affirmative nod from the two white clad figures.

In front of the hole was a pile of rubble and an open black refuse sack that looked to be filled with plaster. As she looked more closer she saw the body in the middle of the pile. She stepped back, shocked raising her hand to her mouth. "Oh sweet Jesus," she looked at Sam. He could see that she was clearly shaken.

He moved forward and knelt to look more closely. He took a sharp intake of breath. He had over the years seen it all. He was close to retirement and felt that there was little left to shock him after so long in the job. He was wrong.

The black refuse sack had been ripped open by Tom, the plumber. He had joked with Carlos that perhaps some one had hidden the family jewels and had forgotten to retrieve them. They had laughed at the idea but the laughter came to an abrupt end when they had looked inside the sack.

Mandy and Sam were looking at the body of a very small baby. It was perfectly preserved. On looking closely Mandy could see that it had the appearance of being mummified,

"Christ, said Sam. They looked at each other in a moment of shock. They were silent for a few moments taking it in and getting their brains to process it. Some one had taken a newly born baby, they could see the remains of the umbilical cord and entombed it in a hole in a wall.

"Pathologist," Sam finally found words.

Mandy for a brief moment found that her legs were not responding and had to will herself to move. They made their way to the front room. It was now clear why the forensics team had been so subdued and taciturn when they had arrived. She signalled for the scientists to start the painstaking examination of the crime scene. That left the Doctor sat on the sofa in the living room making notes on his iPad. She approached him. She recognised him." Doctor Isaacs," she pulled off the latex gloves and extended her hand.

"What can you tell me?"

He spoke in a measured voice but it was clear that he too had been moved by the discovery of such a young infant. "As you can see it is a baby no more than a day or even hours old when she died."

"A girl?" said Sam.

"Yes a baby girl, perfectly formed and almost certainly carried full term."

"Was she still born?" said Mandy.

"I would say she was alive, a normal birth."

"How can you know that?"

"It is an assumption at this stage but the cause of death leads me in that direction."

"I don't understand," said Sam.

"The cause of death was strangulation. You would not need to strangle someone that was already dead."

There was silence in the room, shocked silence. Finally Mandy gathered her wits. "Are you saying that some one gave birth to a perfectly healthy baby girl then strangled her and shoved her in a hole in the wall?"

"It would appear so. My guess is that there was existing damage to the wall and the hole was already there. Someone bought a bag of plaster. They put the left over plaster in the refuse sack with the body. Then they put the sack through hole into the void between the external wall and the internal stud wall and then plastered over it.

"Was this recent, the body seems so intact?"

"The plaster is deliquescent, it absorbs moister. It is a fluke but the body is dessicated. Most of the moisture was extracted by the plaster mix. My guess is the plaster also contains fungicide and anti bacterial properties. In other words the body was more or less accidentalist mummified."

"So when was she murdered, roughly. I know it is hard to be precise with these things."

"Just over six years ago," replied Dr Isaacs.

"That is very precise," Sam said," how come?"

"Not science just observation, the bag of plaster was date stamped by the builders merchant. Of course it could have been purchased months or years in advance but there was another give away. Whoever filled the hole used old news paper. It is shoddy workmanship but gives an accurate date."

"The logical assumption is that the murder had to have taken place before the purchase of the plaster and after the printing of the Newspaper," said Mandy.

"Exactly, I will carry more tests back at the lab," said Isaacs. He left to remove the body, while Sam and Mandy took it in.

They remained in silence for a few moments. Both Sam and Mandy were struggling to come to terms with the situation. The question they both struggled with was, who would murder a new born baby, put her in a bin bag and stick her in a hole in the wall?

Mandy jumped as her mobile phone rang. She fumbled in her bag and eventually held it to her ear. "It's Taylor what's going on there?" The Superintendent sounded stressed almost panicked.

"What do you mean, Sir."

"What do I mean? Are you at the scene? Have you looked outside? There's a circus on the streets. The media is going ballistic, rumour, speculation, they are calling it the house of death, baby murders, mass slaughter. Get out there. Make a statement. Calm the situation, now."

On the street Mandy faced the press. The footage was being beamed instantly around the globe.

"I can confirm that the body of an infant had been discovered. I am unable to release any further details at this stage as our investigations are ongoing." She walked away with further questions being shouted at her.

"Well there is no doubt that whoever committed the murder, wherever they are, will know we have discovered it," said Sam.

Chapter 4

Francis drove along the coast road towards Chania. Despite being October the temperature remained high. She had stopped off for a swim in a small bay on Crete's northern shore. The mountain road wound down towards the town where she now lived. On her left the sea was deep blue. Soon the sun would go down but for now the light danced across the wave tops like a million sparkling diamonds.

She had left England just over two years ago and started afresh. A new start, a new life and she was a new person. She took a deep breath as she viewed the sea and mountains. It was clean, and fresh. Her life was clean and fresh. She felt she was purged.

She had met Lilly in Athens. It had been after a concert. She remembered that moment. For her to remember anything during this period of her life was in itself unusual. It had been a pivotal instant in time. She was high as usual, coke, meth and anything she could get her hands on. Lilly was just sitting in the bar. She was quiet, calm almost serene. Francis was hyper, distracted, staggering and verging on the out of control.

"You are a mess," Lilly said.

For some reason Francis heard those words. She was a mess, a total mess. She needed to be a mess. She did not want reality. She could not face the reality. She wanted to remain in the haze of alcohol and drugs. She could hide there and not face herself. She was twenty six old but felt as though she had lived enough of life.

"Yes I fucking am," she replied plonking herself on the chair next to Lilly. "I'm.." she began to introduce herself.

"i know who you are, everybody knows who you are here. My name is Lilly."

"Please to meet you Lilly," Francis was struggling to focus and speak.

"Why are you doing this to yourself?"

"Why am I doing this to myself? Why, because I am . Because I don't want to be here."

"In Athens?"

"No on this fucking planet, I just want to fly away, disappear, be somewhere else, be some one else," Francis felt tears as she ranted.

Lilly reached out and took her hand and held it gently. "That is sad, so sad."

Through the fog induced by the drugs and drink Francis felt something as she held Lilly's hand. It was a moment of calm and safety. She felt she has found something. Something that meant something. A moment away from the chaos that was her life, a moment of tranquillity, an oasis in a desert of self destruction that was her life.

With hindsight it was clear that hand holding with a complete stranger was hardly the epiphany she had felt at the time. Francis realised that it was more likely a drug induced feeling of love and euphoria. It was real at the time so it mattered not. The drugs or love the effect was the same. Francis fell in love.

She just let Lilly take over. She left that bar, her old life and never went back. She gave herself to Lilly and in return Lilly put her back together. The road had been a hard one but she had come off the drugs. They had found a small Turkish style house in the hills above Chania. It was dilapidated, leaky and neglected. They had started to rebuild, the house and Francis. Both were still a work in progress but nearing completion.

Money was tight but Francis received regular cheques for royalties and Lilly worked in a bar in the town. Lilly was Greek and Francis now had a reasonable command of the language. Despite the word lesbian deriving from a Greek Island, inhabited solely by women, the Cretans were less opened minded than their shared history would have suggested. It did not matter. They kept themselves to themselves and avoided conflict.

Francis drove into the centre of Chania and found a parking place next to the city wall. It was a short walk to the market and shops. At this time of year, the tourists gone the pace of life and parking in particular became easier.

Lilly was not working that evening so Francis decided that she would cook. It was rare for them to get an evening together in the summer months. Lilly worked to the early hours serving the customers in the taverna, Now the season ending she would get home in good time and they would have the winter evenings together.

She had decided on fish. She walked around the old town and along the quayside. Despite the fact Crete was an island there was very little fish available to buy. There were however cabbages, lots a cabbages, big and bigger cabbages. She guessed that it was the cabbage growing season. If she wanted a cabbage she would have been fine. She did not want a cabbage but fish.

It was late in the afternoon. She asked about fish and it was suggested that Lidyl was the best place to shop. She laughed to herself as she made her way to a supermarket where she was less than surprised to discover had an offer on cabbages

Francis had to admit to herself that she was not the best cook going but felt she had made a decent effort at an evening meal. Everything was ready she just had to fry the fish and serve. She checked the time. She was ahead of the game and had just over an a hour before Lilly

21

came back. Time for a bath.

The water was a bit tepid. They lived on a tight budget and made use of the solar powered heater and tank on the roof, to keep costs down. The last few days had lacked the essential ingredient though, the sunshine. They had electricity but the cost soon mounted. She settled for a luke warm bath. They had spent little time together over the summer months with Lilly's long hours so now Francis felt they deserved some together time.

She dressed, applied make up, perfume and checked herself in the mirror. She decided she looked presentable. As the sun set and darkness came, she lit candles. She surveyed her handy work, table laid, food prepared, candlelight and looking sexy. All the boxes ticked for a romantic evening.

She looked at her watch. Lilly would be about another half an hour. She would watch the news back in the UK. She pulled out her laptop from a shelf under the coffee table and connected to the internet. The connection was not the fastest but passable. The BBC overseas news came up.

There seemed nothing but Brexit, the moves by Britain to exit the European Union. It had been in the news fro three years and did not get any more interesting. Eventually the coverage switched from politics, the winter crisis in the health service, the delay and cost overruns of various infrastructure projects, nothing changed. Francis was glad to be away from the whole dreary place.

She was about to turn it off when Eastbourne Pier flashed across the screen. It immediately grabbed her attention. She listened to the commentary.

"The body of a baby was discovered in this building. We do not have full details as yet but sources have confirmed that the infant was entombed in the walls. We go live to the scene where DCI Mandy Pile is about to address the press," commentated the newsreader.

Time froze as Francis viewed the footage. At that moment her world came to a halt. Wherever she thought she was living in space and time became a fantasy. The reality was screaming out to her from the screen of her PC. She knew that it had been a dream. There was no escape from life. In those few minutes her life had come crashing down. She knew that she could no longer hide and pretend. Eastbourne was real and she had to face it.

Hands trembling she picked up her mobile phone. She searched through her contacts and located the number she had not dialled in years. It was a number she hoped never to have to use again, part of another life.

The phone eventually connected and the familiar voice came onto the line. "Have you seen the news? Yes it is me. I cannot hide from this. No, I have decided to go to the police. I know now that cannot live with it."

Chapter 5

There was a tense atmosphere in Eastbourne Police Station. Superintendent Taylor sat in silence n the incident room. Sam Shaw, DC's, Merryweather, Potts and Siskin felt uncomfortable waiting, fully aware of the tension building in the room. Taylor took his phone from his pocket and began distractedly scrolling through it. No one spoke.

Finally after another eight or nine minutes, which seemed to the team like another eight or nine hours the door flew open and Mandy Pile bounced in. "Good morning all," she said removing her coat and throwing her bag on the desk positioned at the head of the room.

Taylor coughed loudly to make his presence known to her. "Oh," she said "And a good morning to you Sir." She smiled and waited for his response.

He ignored the greeting and pointedly looked at his watch. Mandy pointedly ignored the silent reprimand. "Your team," he said indicating Merryweather and Potts

Mandy addressed her team. "Nice to be working with you again." Then turning to Taylor.

"Could we have a word in private?" she said.

Taylor rose and they made their way to the small office that Mandy would occupy. She closed the door. "Sir, that is not a team. I have the murder of a baby to investigate and three detectives. You do understand that the murder occurred about six years ago.? Tracing the occupants of the flat around that time, following up on their subsequent movements and locating them will be a massive undertaking. How is that to be done with no staff?"

"It is not ideal, I agree. Make a start. Get a investigatory plan in place then we can reassess manpower."

"You know that is unrealistic. A case like this will have hundreds of lines of enquiries. Anyone could be crucial. There is a real danger we will overlook something crucial."

"We have the resources we have. We have the officers we have. I cannot give you what is not available. We are not the only force fighting the odds. Everyone is in the same boat, funding cuts and less police dealing with more crime. Don't shoot the messenger Mandy. It is what it is. So please get started and we will take it from there."

Mandy was less than happy but had no other options open to her. "Thanks for clarifying," she said disingenuously.

"Bye the way, why were you late?"

" I was trying to save my shoes."

Taylor starred at her seeking clarification., "I am not with you?"

"When the call came through yesterday I had booked off and was going up to London for a gala dinner at the Savoy. As there was no one else available I had to divert dressed in my going out gear. If you remember it was blowing a gale and peeing down."

"I saw your press interview on the TV. I do remember thinking that you looked very smartly turned and what a credit you were to the Force."

"You are joking I hope?" Taylor gave nothing away remaining stone faced. "That was a designer cocktail dress, designer shoes and top coat.

They were not designed for clambering about building sites, gale force winds and monsoons. They were, however designed to be worn indoors sheltered from the elements in the Savoy ballroom. Having sacrificed all for attending a murder scene I felt I could at least see if I could salvage the shoes."

He rose and leaving, said," okay keep me in the loop with any new developments on the case. And of course your shoes."

"Right boss," said Sam as she rejoined her team."Who do you want doing what?"

"What we have so far is a murdered infant that was hidden behind the stud wall in a flat in Eastbourne. We can tentatively place the time of death in about June 2013 that is to say about six years ago. This is based on items associated with the body, a newspaper and the packaging from a bag of plater. We do not know the identity of the victim."

She turned to the white board on the wall behind her and began to write as she spoke. "First we need to find out who the baby was and her parents. DNA may help but as you know that could be some time coming and then we still have to get a match to identify the parents."

"We need to track down who the tenants of the flat were during that period."

"According to the pathologist at the scene the baby was no more than a few weeks old. So we need to look at all births at home and in hospital around that time. We need to follow up and see if those now six year olds are alive and in school."

She handed over to Sam. "Merryweather, Potts you make a start on the hospitals and midwives." "Siskin dig into the property records and find out who lived there at the time."

Sam and Mandy moved back to the small office. "This is hopeless" said Sam. "We need more detectives. Do you know how many kids are born in the Eastbourne and Brighton area each month?"

"No, tell me," said Mandy.

"I don't know but I am guessing a lot. A lot more than one DC can sift through in a month of Sundays. Then looking at that block of flats, where the baby was found I would hazard a guess that the landlord is not going to be a model record keeper. The place was clearly little more than a doss house, cash in hand, overcrowded, tenants in and out. What are the chances of any meaningful records being kept of who was living there at the time. It would take a dozen detectives months to drill down on who had lived there and when. Then even if we found out,we would still need to track them all down."

"It is the same old. No enough police and not enough money. I asked Taylor and he is doing what he can. We have to get on with it and use what we have available. You enjoy a good moan now, when you have had that, shall we solve the case?" She smiled.

Sam muttered something featuring the words posh and silver spoon and left the room.

Chapter 6

Dr Evens sat opposite Sam and Mandy in his cluttered office at the pathology laboratory. He held a thin file, which he opened and studied before speaking. "You saw the scene and how the body was preserved so there is no need to go over that."

"As to cause of death that is harder to say."

"It could be natural?" said Sam.

"I didn't say that. I said the actual cause was hard to specify. It was murder but there was so much trauma it is hard to distinguish the actual event that led to death."

"The baby was beaten?"

Dr Evens paused before answering. " There was so many breaks and bruises that as I said it is hard to decide which blow caused death. I also need to distinguish the peri and post mortem injuries. Let's not forget the body was entombed and pushed into a small cavity in the wall"

Mandy looked shocked and her hands were beginning to tremble. "How long?"

"Dr Evens interrupted her. "How long did she live, a matter of hours, no longer."

"I am sorry. I am struggling to take this in," said Sam. "Are you saying that some gave birth and within a matter of hours used the newborn as a football?" His voice was shaky as he spoke.

There was silence in the room. Dr Evens did not reply allowing the information he had provided to be absorbed and processed by Mandy and Sam. Finally Mandy tearing her mind away from the dreadful scene painted in her head by the pathologist regained her voice.

"Is there anything else of use you can tell us?" she said.

"Well the date of death as evidenced by the associated material, that is to say the newspaper and packaging is entirely consistent with the state of the remains."

"Identification, DNA?" she followed up.

"I think I have some viable samples and have sent them to the lab. You should get their findings in a very short time. I appended a note explaining the nature of the crime."

Mandy rose and thanked him. Sam didn't move. "Sam, Sam," said Mandy trying to gain his attention.

He looked up at her his mind obviously elsewhere." Sorry what?" he said.

"We are leaving."

"Oh yes, I have a Granddaughter. She was born a few weeks ago. I was just thinking .."

"Don't," said Mandy. "We need to try and stay emotionally detached. It won't do any good to get involved. Now, come on there is work to be done." Sam roused himself and followed her out of the building.

Mandy and Sam stood in the cool outside air in silence for a few moments before making their way to the car. Mandy took the wheel and Sam sat in the passenger seat. "What now?" he said.

"Back to the Nick and see how Siskin is making out with tracking down who was living there at the time."

Siskin as it turned out was making progress but had hit a brick wall. "So there you have it The property was owned by Christos Koumi at the time. I think it was a buy to let."

"Did he provide you with a list of the tenants or the letting agents details?" said Mandy.

"Not that easy, I am afraid. He is a hard man to find. I have tried the usual, driving licensee, passport, tax and criminal record, so far nothing."

"What about the Land Registry and his solicitor? They are required to get a copy of his passport and proof of address before they act for anyone."

"I have contacted them and they have emailed their client file. It seems Mr Koumi was introduced by a third party who did the checks, a firm based in Cypress."

"Are they allowed to do that?" said Sam.

"You really should read the papers, Sam. There seem to be law firms based in Panama that for a fee will create an identity for you and aid you to bypass the money laundering provisions. That way your identity is concealed, you avoid both taxation and scrutiny," said Mandy.

"i don't think this is as sophisticated as that. It seems that this Mr Koumi might have a few bob stashed away in Cyprus and as you say probably dodged tax on it. He then bought a flat in the UK and set it up in such a way to dodge any tax that might be due here."

"Not a criminal master mind then?" said Mandy.

"No just a bit dodgy. I have emailed the law firm in Cyprus and I am waiting for them to get back," said Siskin.

As if on cue Siskin's phone rang. He mouthed. "it's them."

Sam and Mandy listen to the conversation. "I realise that client information is confidential but we are not making enquiries into Mr Koumi's tax affairs. This is a murder investigation." There was clearly a certain amount of protestation from the other end of the phone.

Siskin interrupted, "Enough, you can either get your client to contact us or I shall get a international arrest warrant for murder. I will make sure that your name is on it as a potential suspect,have the local police attend your office and seize every bit of paper they can find. Trust me we will go through what we find with a fine tooth comb. It is up to you? This a murder investigation but how we expand the scope of it is up to us."

They was a pause. "Thank you for your cooperation," smiled Siskin putting the phone down.

"That was impressive," said Mandy.

"I have been watching the American CIS series on the telly. The detective used the same tactic to get some information from a dodgy lawyer on a drug dealer in last nights episode," said Siskin.

"Bit of luck that lawyer in Cyprus doesn't watch it as well. It would take a month of Sundays to get a warrant and I don't think you would get the Cypriot police to start raiding local law firms with no evidence of a crime," said Sam.

"You are such a pessimist," said Mandy.

"They are a commercial law firm not a criminal one. They won't want to get involved with murder. They will give us what we want," said Siskin.

Mandy returned to her office and left Siskin to it. She had hardly sat down and started to sip a coffee when her phone rang. "It's Siskin. I have Mr Christos Koumi on the phone for you, from Cyprus."

Chapter 7

"Okay everybody let's have a bit of hush to let the boss speak," said Sam. Merryweather, Potts and Siskin swivelled their chairs round to face him and Mandy.

She stood in front of the white board which was still mostly white, an indication of the lack of progress so far. "Merryweather, Potts tell me have you made any progress at the local hospitals checking for births around the time our victim was born?"

"Lots of female births," Potts held up a long list. "But tracking them down to see if they are still alive six years on is not so easy."

"To be honest, we need more people," said Merryweather. "It is very labour intensive. Some are straight forward. If the child is at the same address as the one given by the Mother on admission. It is   a phone call to Mum and a check with the child's doctor. Of course people move about, change their names by marriage and so do their children if adopted. Of course some will have died naturally or in accidents. There is no real tie up between the register of births and deaths. People move abroad and people die abroad."

"In short, trying to track a child from a birth record is not a simple task and to be honest we are making little headway," said Potts.

"If the she was borne in a hospital there will be a record," said Sam.

"No ones is arguing against that," said Merryweather. "We are saying that. We have between us tracked done eight births so far. We have over forty from the General Hospital alone and then there is home births and Brighton Hospitals as we expand our search out. With two of us on it it could be months and that is assuming the birth was ever registered."

"Can't you go via the Registry of Births and work back?" said Mandy.

"Thought of that, it does not give us sufficient detail, basically place of birth, say Eastbourne and the parents. We can search by date and it comes up with every child born on a given date but Countrywide. Then we need to narrow it down to location. The problem we cannot specify an exact date other than sometime before 19th June 2013. That's a lot of babies being born up and down the Country. Obviously it is possible but we need more detectives to do it in a reasonable time scale."

"You are right, of course. And it assumes that the birth was in a hospital and then the parents actually registered the birth. Given the circumstances of the girl's death it seems that we are not dealing with loving parents who would be law abiding enough to register the birth," said Mandy.

"What do you suggest?" said Sam.

"I think we have to give up on this approach and tackle the identification from another route. Trying to identify the victim from the Birth or hospital records will just take too long with the manpower we have and given the birth may not have been registered in the first place may make the whole exercise pointless in any event."

"Put it on the back burner and refocus our attentions else where?" said Sam.

"All agreed?" said Mandy. There was a general nodding of heads around the room.

"Any luck with tracking the tenants?" said Sam to Siskin.

"Well I started with the Council Tax records. In theory that tells you who was living there. The theory is one thing and practice another. Lots of County Court Judgements for non payment."

"So you have names?"

"For what it is worth. They are mostly Greek sounding."

"Well do their addresses?"

"There's the problem right there," said Siskin. "The address on the CCJ is the actual flat, typically a Mr Khristadolou or some such. Of course by the time anyone turns up to collect there is no trace of said Mr Khristadolou. It seems the flaw with CCJs is that they are linked to an address. So looking up the records just gives you a list of people at that address who have defaulted on the Council Tax and have CCJs entered against them."

"So you have a name and that is it."

"Waste of time," continued Siskin. "I have a list, of what in the main will be fake names. I can of course search the electoral roles and other databases for that name but that of course just gives me a list of people with the same name and an address which again may or may not be current."

"They don't have this problem on the TV on CSI. They just pop in a name and have the perp's location, phone records, life history, driving license and a photo in minutes," mused Merryweather.

"Perp?" said Sam.

"Perpetrator," said Mandy. "Please stop watching US cop shows. You do know they are not real don't you?"

Merryweather pulled a sad face. " A man can dream."

"Alright given that we don't have unlimited manpower and local authority records are proving about as useful as a pair of swimming trunks to a dessert nomad. We have to work with what we have and you will be glad to hear that you esteemed lead has come to your aid,"

said Mandy.

She continued. "I have just come off the phone to the person that owned the flat during the period of interest. Mr Koumi albeit reluctantly admitted he let the flat out and received rent at the time despite not showing said income on his tax returns. So we have a name, Mr Rod Hardy."

"And joy of joys the lab has moved quickly and we have the DNA profile back. They have managed to get a viable sample from the baby girl."

"Right now we have some leads at last. Track down Mr Hardy and see if we can match the DNA and locate the victim's parents."

Chapter 8

Mandy felt a little more hopeful of getting somewhere even with the limited resources to hand. She had just finished a phone call to Superintendent Taylor. Sam had sat quietly in her office listening to the exchange.

"You heard that?" she said.

"I got the drift, the calvary is on the way but not just yet. A number of investigations are winding down, more man power available soon, blah, blah, blah.."

"Succinctly put, I was hoping with the DNA and our potential suspect, Rod Hardy, given to us by our Cypriot friend, that he would see the investigation stepping up a gear. It is what it is though it will just take us a bit longer, that's all."

"It is frustrating though and it does make it harder. It is the knock on effect while you plough through lists of names, car registrations or list of whatever you have to be totally focussed so as not to miss something but that means you cannot look at the bigger picture."

"I don't disagree. It is easy to get lost in the detail and overlook the obvious even when it is starring you right in the face."

"When I was a kid and I grizzled, say as a result of stubbing my toe, my Dad would clip me round the ear," said Sam.

Mandy looked at him slightly horrified. " Apart from the obvious the clear assault, I seem to missing the point of that."

"Well I am just illustrating the point." he said. "Having clipped me around the lug hole. I would say something like, ouch that hurt."

"As you would,"

"Right but my Dad would say 'but your toe doesn't'. That's the same thing I forgot about my toe because of the pain to my head. It is the same. You can't think of two things at once."

"That is not because your Dad was keen on causing you brain damage. The reason you cannot think of two things at once. is simple. You are a man," she said with no hint of sarcasm.

Sam began to speak. Mandy raised her eyebrows and he thought better of it. He left the office with his customary under the breath muttering. This time she could hear words like "good hiding, no harm, kids today."

Sam took up his spot in the main office and hit the computer. All hands were set to the two tasks in hand, getting a match for the DNA from the victim and tracking down the tenant of the flat at the time Rod Hardy.

Hours passed and frustration levels rose. The landlord had been unable to provide any details of his tenant apart from the name. The rent was paid in cash, which suited Mr Koumi but was of no help to the team.

"Are you sure that Koumi didn't just pluck a name out of the air to get you off his back?" said Siskin.

"I don't think so. When I said there was the death of a baby involved he was upset. He may not like paying tax but he definitely did not like the idea of child murderers. No my gut feeling was that he genuinely wanted to help."

"The problem is that without a middle name and a full first name it is hard to narrow the search sufficiently to make it meaningful."

"So what are you searching?"

"Hardy R," said Siskin.

"Let's make a few assumption. Firstly we need to narrow the age. Koumi said the chap was in his late twenties. So today we need to look say thirty to forty years old, giving us a date of birth of say 1979 to 1989."

"Okay and the most obvious Christian name is Rodney."

"That can't be that many people who would call the kids Rodney," joked Mandy.

"I know this might seem an odd question but do you watch television at all?" he said.

"What's that supposed to mean. Have you jumped on the Sam theory of me that I am too posh to flush my own toilet?" She was smiling.

"Are you, joke, joke?" he said quickly. "Well have you ever watched a TV comedy show called Only Fools and Horses?"

It was clear that she had not."What channel is it on?"

"No it was on in the eighties."

"How old do you think I am?" said Mandy becoming annoyed.

"Everyone watches the reruns. I am only a bit older than you," he hastily added, "I am guessing at age of course and I watch them."

Mandy was beginning to wonder where this was leading. "Is there a point to this?"

"Oh yes, Rodney was a major character in the TV show. I was pointing out that there might be a hell of a lot more Rodney's than you would think in that time frame. Just saying," he trailed off as Mandy gave him her get on with it look.

"So ignoring popular TV shows we should start local Eastbourne, Brighton etcetera and work out. Narrow by date of birth and then hit the electoral rolls and the rest." She walked over to Potts and Merryweather.

"Any luck?"

"I have been going through police records searching for partial matches. We have Mitochondrial DNA which comes from the mother. Looks like she had no criminal record or at least no sample of DNA was taken if she did." Potts.

"Any ideas?" she asked Merryweather.

"Well I was watching CSI.."

"What is going on here? Everyone on the team seems addicted to some TV soap or other"

Merryweather ignored her. "As I was saying I was watching CSI and they identified someone where they had been a victim of a crime and their DNA had been taken to eliminate them from the investigation."

"Where did that take you?" asked Mandy.

"I decided not to search the criminal data base but victims whose DNA should not be on file still which as we know sort of is."

"And?" she said.

"Any minute now." They watched as the screen showed the usual spinning circle letting them know at least something was happening.

There was an awkward silence as they waited. The computer let out an audible chime signifying a hit.

"Eureka we have a match," said Merryweather, " Millicent Nook."

.

Chapter 9

Mandy felt that with the DNA match matters were at last moving in the right direction. The next step would be to track down the mother of the baby girl and bring her in for questioning. She had left Potts to contact Birmingham Nick and get the details of why Millicent Nook was in the system. They still needed to find the father who also might be implicated in the child's death. The man with the answers of who was also living in the flat at the time was the as yet untraced, Rod Hardy.

She made her way to where Siskin, sat at his desk and was busy tapping on his computer keyboard. "Anything?" she asked.

"Yes but still too much." She lent over as he scrolled down the list of Hardies. "Narrowing the age helps but it still leaves forty to fifty likely candidates countrywide. If we come to this area we have a couple but they look highly unlikely to be honest."

"Give me their addresses. Sam will pay them a visit. You never know."

The drive to Hailsham a few miles outside of Eastbourne proved to be quite pleasant. The rain and gusting wind had finally stopped. On the other hand Sam had not and was still in a moaning frame of mind. They were driving on a stretch of dual carriage way and stuck behind a tractor. The inside lane had been taken out of the equation by a endless row of traffic cones. "Can you see anybody?" He answered his own question. "No you can't. Is any body actually doing any road works.? No

40

they are not. I am sure it is a job creation scheme. They employ some one to put cones out in the morning and then they employ some one to pick them up in the evening."

Mandy laughed. "I am sure they have a plan and it is not just a plot to annoy you."

"You are wrong there. It is definitely a plan to annoy me and anyone else that actually might be doing some work rather than cone moving about." He grunted.

They eventually turned off and made their way down a few twisty lanes to their destination, 'Hardy Antiques Centre.' The Centre was located in some converted farm buildings. A series of out buildings and barns had been re-purposed as teas rooms, and a space housing a number of antique dealers and craft sellers.

"This looks very nice," said Mandy as Sam pulled up in the gravel car park.

Sam grunted and headed to the door marked entrance. Mandy in her high heels struggles to maintain balance on the uneven surface. He pushed the door open and held it waiting for her to catch up. They made their way inside the building and passed a number of stalls. There was no one to be seen.

"A hive of activity," he said before shouting loudly. "Anyone at home?"

Mandy jumped. "Warn me the next time you intend to start shouting your head off."

They heard a rustling from further inside and a small man, dressed in corduroy trousers and a cardigan appeared from behind, of what seemed to Mandy and Sam, some old junk. "Can I help?" He asked as he emerged from the mountain of junk, peering through the thick lenses of his spectacles.

"We are looking for a Mr Rodney Hardy?"

"That is I. How can I help you?"

"Sam produced ID. "This is DCI Pile and I am DS Shaw. We would like to ask you some questions."

"If it's about the jewellery, I already told your collogues that I had no idea it was stolen.."

"This is in connection with a completely different matter," said Sam.

"Do you know a Millicent Nook?" asked Mandy.

"I am pretty sure I don't. Of course I don't know the names of all the customers. So I can't say for definite."

"I meant on a personal level?"

"Oh no definitely not. I have never met anyone of that name."

"Have you ever rented a flat in Eastbourne?" said Sam.

"No never I have lived here in Hailsham all my life apart from when I went to University in Guildford."

Sam looked at Mandy. She could see by his expression that he was of much the same opinion as her. This Mr Rodney Hardy could be more or less ruled out. They would get his history checked out but for now there was little more to be said.

"That was a waste of time," said Sam.

They drove in silence until they reached the dual carriage way. "You are kidding me," said Sam. They had removed the cones from the north bound stretch and were now laying them southbound. "I am sure they are definitely targetting me."

Mandy settled back for a moaning session until they reached their next port of call.

"Right, number two Rodney on the list," said Mandy as they pulled up at the address given to her by DC Siskin.

"Why do I feel this is another waste of time?" said Sam.

"Because you are a negative kind of guy," said Mandy.

"No because this is a care home."

"He is to young to be a resident," she pointed out.

"Yes but not too young to be the manager," he pointed to the staff profiles on the wall in the reception area, where they were waiting.

"Mr Hardy?" said Mandy as a well dressed man entered the lobby.

"Dr Hardy," he extended his hand. "How may I help you?"

Mandy and Sam were back in the car after five minutes heading back to the Police Station. " I told you that it would be a waste of time," moaned Sam.

"They had to be eliminated though."

"Let's hope they have made better progress with locating the baby's mother, Millicent Nook."

Back in the incident room they called the team together and updated them on the progress or lack there of in finding Rod Hardy. "Now who is going to give me some good news?" said Mandy.

"I have an idea that might help us track down Mr Hardy," said Siskin. "I phoned Mr Koumi the ex owner of the flat and asked him if he thought he would be able to identify Mr hardy from a photo. He seemed pretty confident that he could. So I have done the obvious. I have trolled through the various social media platforms looking for profiles under that name."

"With what results?"

"I have come up with a pile of photos a people called Rodney, Rod, Ronald and Ronaldo Hardy. I have sent Mr Koumi a link and as we speak he is looking through them for his ex- tenant."

"Well done let's hope he comes up trumps for us. Now where are with Millicent Nook? Do we have an address, her current whereabouts?"

Potts and Merryweather both began to speak at once. "You talk," said Potts.

Merryweather started talking again. "We have received the files and we have been trying to piece things together. Can we double check our understanding of the pathology report before we continue?"

"Go on," said Sam.

Potts looked down at a piece of paper he held in his hand. "Is there anyway that the baby girl died earlier than the dates we have been given."

"The evidence is pretty strong and matches the autopsy results. We can be almost certain that death occurred in June 2013, why?"

"Because Millicent died on the 15th October 2012, eight months before the baby was killed," he said. "Given the fact that the baby was only days old, she was already dead when she was supposed to have given birth."

Chapter 10

He had not slept well. The rolling of the ferry had made him feel queasy. The background noise of the engine and the vibrations from it had given him a headache. It was five in the morning and the ferry from Athens was not due to dock for at least another hour and a half. He made his way onto the deck and the fresh air. It surprised him that it was still dark. There was a hint of the morning sunrise on the horizon but the new day was not yet ready to put in an appearance. He took a few gulps of the sea air and made his way back inside.

The ferry was half empty. The tourist season was more or less at an end and the Greek Island hoping tourists had departed. The boat was was mainly filled with locals and the goods that needed transporting to the Island to stock the shops and bars on Crete. The lorry drivers were beginning to stir and move around the boat. They mostly knew each other and would share a journey back later that day to the mainland.

He ordered coffee and sat watching the daybreak and the Island growing larger as they approached. He had taken him a long time to get to Crete, much longer than the four hours it would have taken by plane from Heathrow. He had travelled to Paris. Then book a flight to Athens. Arriving he had taken the train to Piraeus port and paying cash, bought his ticket to Heraklion, the capital of Crete. Placing him on the island would be hard for any interested party.

Eventually the ferry docked and he made his way from the quayside. It did not take him long to locate what he was looking for. A small hotel, slightly shabby and not part of a chain. The sort of hotel where paying in cash was appreciated. He booked a room for the night. He intended to take the ferry back to Athens the following morning.

The hotel had an internet connection. He checked the flight arrival times from England. There were no delays. He had phoned two days before from a newsagent that provide an internet phone service for foreign nationals living in the UK. It was used mostly by illegal workers to contact their families back home. It was not only cheap but anonymous.

He had given details of a flight arriving later that day and asked her to meet him at the airport. He had no intention of taking the flight and his name would not appear on any manifest flying to Crete. He knew the ferry took your money and sold you a ticket. They did not ask for ID. No one knew or could trace him to Crete.

Having confirmed the plane, he was supposedly on, was on time, he took the bus to the airport. He sat on his suitcase, outside Arrivals and waited. He did not have to wait long. She was walking towards him past the row of buses, coaches and hotel pickup vehicles. He stood up and moved towards her arms outreached in preparation for a hug.

"Francis," he said joyously and hugged her closely. Her car was parked a few minutes walk away. He noticed that there were parking restrictions in force. She like most of the other cars had ignored them. He put his case in the boot and they began to drive towards Rethymnon on the northern coastline. "I know a lovely taverna with great views, lunch?" she smiled.

She had not been lying the restaurant sat on the side of a hill, with the dining room affording panoramic views across the now deep blue sea and rocky bay. The cliffs feel steeply down to the bay. "It is beautiful," he said.

"That's why I moved here. I had enough. I needed something fresh, something untarnished."

"Tell my about Lilly?"

"She has changed my life. For once I feel that I have something of my own. Someone to love, someone who wants me and not what I represented."

He looked out into the distance and seem to go to a far away place in time. "We all wanted that. Most of us never found it. You say you have so why would you want to destroy it?"

"Because it is a lie. It is all lies. It is vile and nothing any of us can do will put it right."

"But what good would it do? You will just destroy more lives. Who would it benefit?"

"Me, it would benefit me." She had tears in her eyes and her hand trembled as she took a cigarette and lit it. The taverna owner brought over an ashtray, Cretans were very relaxed over parking and smoking laws.

"It is not just you though is it. You going to the police will destroy more than just your life."

"I won't give names."

"You are being naïve. The police are not stupid. They will dig until they get the truth. What about Lilly?"

The tears were now filling her eyes. "I know, I know and I love her so but.."

"But you are going to throw it all away to ease your conscious ?"

"It is more than that. You know that. What happened was wrong. It was was worse than that it was evil."

He turned his attention back to the sea below. There were a number of small boats sailing in the bay. He took one of Francis' cigarettes and lit it. He took a deep breath and blew the smoke out slowly, almost a sigh, a sigh of resignation. He turned back and faced her. "You are set on this, no matter the consequences?"

She nodded. He stood up and walked to her side of the table. Kneeling before her he cupped her face in his hands. He held her there affectionately and kissed her gently. "Have you told anyone else about this?"

"No only you, I knew you would understand that you of all people would be with me."

"What about Lilly, does she know you are meeting with me? Have you prepared her?"

"No she knows nothing. I waited for you. We need to do this together."

"You are right, together," he said.

Chapter 11

"So you have had time to read the files on Millicent Nook," said Sam. "So tell us all about it. We are sitting comfortably."

Mandy had gathered the team together in the incident room so that they would all be up to speed. " Right, Merryweather we need an over view and then I shall break it down for further analysis. Let's all see the bigger picture."

"It starts with a call to the Fire Service at approximately four o'clock in the morning on the 15th October 2012. Which is coincidently almost seven years to the day that the baby's body was found here in Eastbourne buried in the wall of the flat."

He began reading the call log from the emergency number. "The caller was driving to work from Coventry to Birmingham. He drove the same route each morning at that time to his place of employment at a bespoke artisan baker in Birmingham. There were no other cars on the road."

"Surely a quicker route would be the motorway?" said Siskin.

"The local Police checked it all thoroughly by the look of it. The place of work was on an industrial estate and the witness lived on the outskirts. It may have been slight faster taking the main route but longer mileage. The witness made the journey seven days a week starting work at five and finishing at around lunchtime. The slightly longer time was more than adequately compensated for by the saving on petrol."

"Makes sense," said Siskin.

"Did they check out the witness movements?" said Potts.

"Yes completely ruled out of any involvement. So the emergency services log the call. Essentially the caller see an abandoned car that seems to have come off the road and has burnt out. Because the witness drives the route everyday, he knew that this is a recent event. His assumption is that the car has been stolen the night before, and crashed by the kids who nicked it. In order to destroy the evidence, they have set it on fire and legged it."

"The police seem to have taken the same view. They establish that the car is well off the road and there is no danger to traffic. The are still dealing with the fall out from the night before, drunks, fights the usual. The fire service are informed but as the car is not a danger and the fire is out they mark it a non urgent."

"So how long before anyone attends the incident?" said Mandy.

"They get there at six thirteen."

"When it gets light."

"That would seem to be the case, yes."

"Okay go on."

"That's when they discover that there is a body lying in the foot well in the rear of the car."

"And that's when they finally get their arses in gear and started to pay attention," said Sam.

"A bit harsh," said Mandy. "We have to make judgment calls everyday. Don't forget most burglaries reported here are not even followed up by a visit unless there is a good chance we might have a chance of nicking someone for it. I assume that they are as under resourced as we are."

Merryweather continued. "They recover the body of a young woman." He skipped a few pages. "Here it is the pathologists report. Right so the body is that of a young female burnt beyond recognition."

"Anything else in the car?" said Potts.

"Nothing else is recovered from the vehicle, no prints, no personal items, no nothing. They identify the vehicle from the chassis number and trace the registered keeper. When the Police go to the address where the car is registered the owner is still in bed. He was unaware that the vehicle was missing and is shocked to see it still not parked where he left it the previous day. A note here says that the estate is a hot spot for taking and driving, kids mostly looking for a bit of excitement."

"It a national pastime. Nick a car and have a laugh," said Sam.

"I have the Fire Service investigator's report here. They looked at the pattern of the fire as it spread through the vehicle. It concludes that the car was not set on fire but that it burst into flames soon after impact. The fuel tank was ruptured and petrol leaked. The positioning of the tank meant that vapour leaked into the interior of the car. They have no way of being certain but the obvious cause of the petrol turning to a gas or vaporising rapidly would be application of heat from either the brakes, if the car had been braking violently or the exhaust system."

"So the petrol fumes filled the car soon after it crashed?" said Mandy.

"Yes and any spark would have ignited it. The Fire Officer could not pinpoint the exact cause of ignition but as it say in the report there are a considerable number of electrical based systems in a modern car and any one could have shorted as result of the impact."

"So the car crashes and burst into flames?" said Sam.

"Not immediately, not like the classic scene in the movies where the car goes over the cliff and explodes on impact with the ground. There was more time than that. The car comes off the road, the petrol tank is ruptured and then the fuel vaporises on the exhaust and the passenger area is filled with petrol vapour. The report is not precise as to how long the interval was after the crash and the car cashing fire bit it was not instantaneous."

"So the assumption is that the driver and any other occupants make it out before the car catches fire?" said Mandy.

Exactly," said Merryweather. "Except Millicent Nook, who does not make it."

"We can picture the scene easily enough. A group of drink or drug impaired teenagers think they will round off a night out on the town with a bit of a laugh. They steal a car and race it around the country lanes. The joy ride turns into a tragedy when it crashes. They stagger from the wreckage all except Millicent Nook, that is. Before they can do anything or perhaps realise that she is not with them the car goes up in flames," said Mandy.

"That's about it," said Merryweather.

"So how did they identify her?"

"She was too badly burnt for a visual. I dont have the full lab report but it was by DNA."

"So there is no doubt that it is Millicent Nook," said Mandy.

"Well how the hell did she give birth to a baby months later? That is not possible."

"Identical twin?" siad Siskin.

"No twin I am afraid,"

"There has to be anexplaination," said Mandy. "Let me think on it. Get the full report on my desk and get all the evidence from the Midlands Force out of their storage and down here."

"There is a bit more to report before we all wander off" said Potts.

"Go on."

"Mr Koumi our Greek friend, the landlord of the flat has come up trumps. He had indentified a photograph from those I harvested from social media and emailed him. We have our Rod Hardy, the tenant of the flat when the baby was killed."

Chapter 12

"It is so beautiful up here, don't you think?" said Francis. They sat high above Suda Bay, Below the boats looked like toys in a bath tub. The Sun was going down and the deep red of evening spread across the water. There was still the sound of crickets chirping and the smell of pine lingered on the air.

"It is truly peaceful," he replied.

They had finished their meal and she had driven him on a tour of the Island. They had parked high on the cliffs and leaving the car had settled to view the sunset. "What made you leave it all behind?"

"Lilly I suppose and a need for space. I needed to distance myself from the claustrophobic world we inhabited at that time."

"It was coming to an end anyway, I suppose," he said.

"The whole experience sucked me dry. It took everything that was me and destroyed it. It left me drained, addicted and broke. Lilly found me a husk. I was completely empty inside. I felt that I had been used. No, we had all been used. We were just a cash cow to be milked. We had every last drop squeezed out of us and then we were dumped."

"It is how the music industry is. We were naïve and trusted the wrong people. It is not a new story. You have a new life here. You are content. Why rake over the past?"

"Guilt, the need for redemption a need for absolution, I don't really understand it myself. I want to be the whole me again. As it stands it will always be a dark corner of my life, always there wanting to be exposed, waiting for a light to be shone onto it."

"It was not your fault. Things happen, we were all so high that most of the time we did not know what we were doing."

"Is that really a justification, It was a choice to live like that. I made that choice. For whatever reason I went down that path. Nobody made me. I did it to myself. Having reached that place does it excuse what happened? "

He looked out at the sunset and did not reply. What could he say? Everything she had said was right but he did not want to revisit the past. He did not want to be held to account. It was behind him. He had moved on. Seven years was a long time and things change. He had changed. His life had changed.

They had been famous, briefly and then it passed. It had almost destroyed Francis but it had opened doors for him. He had taken advantage of the opportunity. He had a good life and he wanted to keep it.

"Do you make any money from it now?" he said.

"A pittance," she responded.

"But you wrote everything."

"I know that. All of you know that but I only own a tiny percentage the rest was stolen, like most of what we earned."

"Would money make the difference? I could talk to the others and come to arrangement?"

She looked at him and realisation began to permeate her understanding. "Why are you here?" Really why are you here?"

"I told you I am here to support you."

She stood up and felt the anger rising. "That's not true is it? You have been sent to buy me off, to shut me up, you bastard?"

He tried to remain calm and regain control of the dialogue. "Look it was in the past. It was unfortunate.."

"That does not make it right. It is now and will be there forever. They have found the body. It was all over the news."

"But what good would it really do, you going to the police? We have moved on. We have lives that are different. We are different," he said.

"You fucking heartless bastard, do you think that is how it works? Whoops there's a dead person, never mind, forget that and carry on. Is that what you think? Never mind I am okay. Never mind I have a nice life, really, really."

She was becoming increasingly angry. He tried to calm matters. "You have to be reasonable.."

"Reasonable, what you want is far from reasonable. It was senseless, selfish, irrational, disgusting, barbaric if fact it was a lot of things but it was not fucking reasonable."

He stepped towards her and gripped her arms, pinning them to her side. He pushed his face close in to hers. "Listen to me, do you expect us to let you destroy all our lives? What gives you the right? It happened. It was unfortunate but things happen. Nobody meant it to happen."

"Let go of me," she screamed hysterically and tried to pull away.

"Please see reason, we can sort something."

"Fuck you, fuck you," she shouted into his face.

His anger rose and he pushed her away. He pushed hard. He pushed her towards the cliff edge. He pushed her over the edge. He saw the look of realisation of what he had done to her spread across her face as he watched her drop to the rocks below.

He tried to convince himself as he looked down on her smashed body below that he not intended this, that he come to Crete to persuade her not to go to the police. He knew it was just another lie he

56

would tell himself. He knew that it would come to this. He had taken the precautions to disguise his travel from the UK because he had known all along that he had no intention of letting her destroy his life. He knew all along that the stupid bitch would never listen to reason. She never would so he did what had to be done.

He took her car and drove back to Heraklion and took great pains to wipe the car down of figure prints and as much trace of himself being in it as possible. At some stage they would find her body. With luck they would think she had fallen. They would find her car of course but he would be long gone on the ferry. He had left no evidence of his being on ever being on the Island.

Chapter 13

The car turned left at the roundabout and headed past the Langley Shopping centre. Sam was driving and Mandy sat reading a file in the passenger seat. It was still raining as it been for nearly three days. Eastbourne was not living up to its reputation as the Sunshine Coast, far from it.

"My doctors is down that road," said Sam as they pulled up at the mini roundabout. "That reminds me I should get a flue jab. It is that time of year."

"You get them for free. Don't you?"

"How bloody old do you think I am?"

"Oh I didn't know I just thought.."

"Thank you so much," he was quite indignant."That's made me feel a whole lot better." He began to mutter under his breath as he drove towards Mrs Emma Nook's house.

Mandy decided that this was a good time to bury her head in the file DC Potts had put together for her. Millicent's mother Emma still lived in Eastbourne. It was a difficult situation. Her daughter had run away from home and then she was killed in a car crash near Birmingham, a couple of months later.

"What are you going to say?"

Mandy rubbed her eyes with her fingers and let out a long sigh. "I honestly don't know. As far as her Mother is concerned her daughter has been dead for seven years. We have no proof that she did not die in the car crash but on the other hand we do know that she gave birth sometime after. The assumption is that she was still alive and there must have been a mistake somewhere."

"But the DNA is pretty compelling evidence. There is a remote possibility that two people have identical DNA but it is in the millions to one range," said Sam.

"It is not a realistic consideration. The only time there is real doubt with DNA as evidence is usually in the handling or the chain of evidence."

"Cross contamination in the collection or in the lab," said Sam.

"Exactly, the probability of two people having the same DNA is virtually zero. So despite the evidence that she must have been alive I am left with a dilemma. Do I tell her Mother that we suspect Millicent did not die in the car crash or not?"

"It is even more difficult. Even if the evidence suggests she did not die then and subsequently gave birth, do you tell her that her granddaughter was murdered and that her daughter is the prime suspect?"

"We cannot even be sure that Millicent is still alive. It is a nightmare however you look at it."

"This is the house," said Sam. The road was chock a block with parked cars. Sam finally found a space They walked down the road past the parked cars to a small ex-Coucil, terraced house on the estate. "So what are you going to say?"

They had phoned ahead and Mrs Nook was expecting them. She had clearly been looking out. The door opened as they walked up the path. Sam explained who they were and showed his idea. They were taken into a small living room. There were a lot of photos of Millicent around the room, on the wall, on a sideboard and on the window ledge. There were pictures of her as baby, a toddler, at primary school and finally as a teenager. There they stopped. The story of her life came to a sudden stop and there were no more photos.

They sat in an uncomfortable silence for a brief moment while Mandy considered how to start the conversation. Emma finally spoke." They said this has something to do with Millicent?"

"It is in relation to her death. We are re-examining the case," said Mandy.

"You have found the driver responsible for her death?"

"No we are looking at the case in the hope of generating further leads. I am sure that you are aware that there are always advances in forensics that can sometimes help develop the evidence. I just want to review the case at the stage with fresh eyes, so to speak."

"I see," Emma seemed somewhat deflated. Mandy was aware that the woman sat before had lived with the loss of her daughter and the uncertainty of her death for years. Mandy realised that the woman sat before her was in her early forties. She would have been a young girl herself when she had given birth to Millicent.

"It would help if you could go over the events with me. I know that this will be hard for you but it might help?"

Emma sat thoughtfully and gazed out of the window and then at the drips running down the pane. She took a deep breath and turned back facing the detectives. "Okay," she said.

"In the notes it says that Millicent went missing from home?"

"It was more complex than that. I became pregnant with Millicent when I was sixteen. Tom, her father was seventeen but we decided to marry. It was a struggle of course being so young with a baby but we stuck with it. I eventually qualified as nurse and Tom as an accountant. Things improved financially. In truth we grew apart. We were such different people than we had been when we married. We had been together twelve years. Things just fell apart."

"How so?" coaxed Mandy.

"In truth it was me. I met someone else. John. The story writes itself from there. Tom found out and left. There was a messy divorce and I ended up living here with Millicent and John."

"What happened to Tom?"

"He paid his child support but moved up North. The money kept coming but he just completely severed contact not only with me but also with Millicent."

"Had they been close?" said Mandy.

"That had been inseparable. She was a real daddy's girl. The problem was that Tom having found out that I had cheated on him with John took it into his head that Millicent was not his. He convinced himself that I had been with other men before we married."

"Had you?"

"I had been a bit wild in my teens but Tom was definitely Millicent's dad."

"But he no longer believed that?"

Correct, anyway he never bothered to maintain contact, no visits, no phone calls and not even card on her birthday. When John moved in matters got worse. She hated him. It did not matter what he did or how he tried. she would have none of it."

"What age was she when this happened/"

"Twelve thirteen, it was a difficult time. She also had the move from primary school to secondary. She struggled to fit in. She found it hard to make friends. I think there was some bullying involved. I did not really pick up on it, what the split and my new relationship. I blame myself. I should have put her first but I was wrapped up in the situation."

"So talk me through the events," said Mandy.

" Millicent become more and more isolated and distant. She would skip school, disappeared for days. Appear often drunk or under the influence of drugs. She was out of control. The arguments became more and more extreme. It was a constant battle between her and John."

"And you, how was your relationship? Did you know where she was going? Who she was hanging out with? Where she was staying?"

"She hated me I think. She blamed me for her father going. She saw it as I had just got rid of him and stuck John in his place."

"I see, where is John now? Is he living here?"

"That's the irony he had another woman on the go all the while, in fact several. It's true what they say, what goes around comes around. He cleared off a few months after Millicent disappears"

"So he disappeared from the picture. Take me through what happened with Millicent."

"As I said, she had taken to not going to school and was into the drug scene in the Town. When she did not return I reported it to you."

"She had been missing for three days before you contacted us."

"She was out of control by then and her behaviour was erratic. It was not the first time she had disappeared and not the first time the police had been involved."

"Social services?" said Sam.

"Totally useless and that didn't surprise me. As a nurse I have made referrals in the past. They don't have the time or the resources. They tick a few boxes and cover the basis. It is more damage limitation rather than help. There is a serious lack of support for young people with well being and mental issues."

"Did you see here again?"

"No nothing she seemed to vanish. The next thing that happened was a police officer arrived here and sitting me down. She then told me that Millicent had been found in the wreckage of a car in the Midlands."

"Did she know people there, relatives or friends?"

"I told the Police at the time. I knew of no one, or any reason for her to be there. Somehow she had left here and ended up in Birmingham."

"Has anything come to mind subsequently. Have you heard anything from here after she left?" said Sam.

Emma Nook looked puzzled. "No, how could I ? She is dead?"

Chapter 14

It was eight am the following morning when Sam and Mandy met up outside Eastbourne Railway Station. The rain had stopped. There was still twenty minutes before their train left for Victoria Station in London. Sam made his way to the cafe on the concourse and ordered a mug of tea and a bacon butty. Mandy settles for a skinny latte.

"Did you order extra grease with that," she asked?

"Do they do that? I wish I had known. I would definitely have ordered it." Sam bit into the bun and then wiped the juice from his chin. I like a day out in London."

Mandy pulled a face that mimicked being sick before taking a sip of her coffee. "Try not to get the grease all down your tie. We can try and at least look a bit professional."

Sam grunted and ignoring her carried on eating. They were on their way to interview Rod Hardy, Mr Koumi's cash in hand tenant. "I thought Merryweather was going to interview this bloke yesterday when we were talking with Emma Nook?"

"Turns out Mr Hardy was out of the Country for a few days and got back late last night. Knowing how much you like a train ride I thought we would do it today. Talk of the devil that's our train." She jumped up. Sam followed her as she made her way across the Station.

The journey to London was slow and the train packed. They were lucky and had a seat. Sam immediately fell asleep and Mandy busied herself on social media."Wake up," she gave Sam a nudge as they entered the station.

They made their way to the underground and after another half an hour found themselves walking up Waldour Street. "This was where it all happened in the sixties and seventies. All the promoters, agents and song writers did their business here. It was the Tin Pan alley of London," said Sam.

"Not a clue what you are talking about," said Mandy. "Here we are, Rod Hardy Promotions Limited." They had stopped outside a building with about fifteen plastic plaques on the wall, listing the occupants,

On the third floor, they entered the office. The room had been divided into areas. In the first, as you entered their were two females sitting opposite each other with phones and a computer each. The far side led to an office with name Rod Hardy painted on the door.

"Mr Hardy," said Mandy.

"Do you have an appointment?" one of the women replied in an indifferent singsong voice while not looking up. "Mr hardy doesn't see anyone without and appointment. You can make an appointment by going online at Rodhardy dot.."

Sam brought the rehearsed diatribe to an abrupt halt. "I don't need an appointment. Show me in now or I'll drag you all down the Nick for a quick game of twenty questions." He pushed his warrant card under her nose. She stopped typing. He now had her attention.

"You should have said you were the police."

She looked up from her desk and shouted, making Mandy and Sam start. "Rod, the Old Bill are her to see you." Turning back to Mandy and Sam, she said in her original indifferent, sing song voice. "Mr Hardy will see you now. Please go through." She then retuned to her computer.

"We are to talk to you about a property you rented in Eastbourne approximately seven years ago," said Mandy as she and Sam settled into chairs on the opposite side of the desk to Rod Hardy. The walls of his office were peppered with posters and photos of various rock bands, rappers and various singers. They all bore the prominent wording, 'Rod Hardy Promotions'.

"I don't recall renting in Eastbourne."

Sam exhaled loudly in a signal of his annoyance. "Are you really going to try and mess us about Mr Hardy. I am not renowned for my patience and if you come the old soldier with me and make my life harder you can be sure that I will get your life turned over so thoroughly that you will be facing charges for the next hundred years. So how would you like this done, the easy way or the hard way?"

Mandy was slightly taken aback, herself by Sam's old school approach. She realised that despite his curmudgeonly slightly dishevelled outward appearance he was hard as nails, He had been around the block a few times and knew how to give as good as he got.

"There is no need for that," said Rod. "You understand that a man in my position needs to be careful."

"We are not here about a bit of tax dodging. We are investigating a murder," said Sam.

Rod attitude changed. "Oh I see. How can I help.?"

"The flat you rented in Eastbourne, do you remember it now?" said Mandy.

"Clearly," he said.

"So did you live there? Who lived there with you say in 2012 and 2013?"

"I never lived there. I rented another apartment in the Old Town. I had an an arrangement with a Greek bloke, cash in hand."

"Cypriot," said Mandy.

"As I said I paid this bloke cash in hand. The place was not really up to standard and there was no way any respectable letting agent could let it out . It was a bit of a dump really."

"So why did you rent it if you already had a place to live?"

"Well it was cheap and no paper work."

"That wasn't the question. I meant what was your purpose in renting it," she said

"Oh, I see. Well at the time I was trying to get a foothold in the music industry. My idea was to get a band together and see if I could get them a record deal and mange them."

"I assume by the posters on the wall that you have had some success in that area," said Sam

"It took a while but eventually yes. Back then it was a struggle getting anyone's attention."

"Why Eastbourne not the epicentre of the music industry, is it?"

"It sort of fell that way. I finished a course at Brighton University in Music Technology and knew a few friends in the area. Originally I wanted to work in a recording studio and eventually become a headline producer. That didn't happen and I ended being a sound engineering getting regular work in the theatres in the area and venues that put on live bands."

"But you did not give up on becoming an impresario?" said Mandy.

"I started putting on local bands at the venues I worked at. Gradually I built up a steady income as a local promoter. It was okay but I knew I needed to do something more if I wanted a real living. So I decided to sign and manage a pop band,."

"The flat?"

"Somewhere to house them and keep them together while I pushed the music."

"So who was living there at the time?" pushed Sam.

"Is this something to do with that baby's body found in Eastbourne? I saw it on the news."

Sam and Mandy said nothing.

"Oh shit, it was found in the flat?" Rod's face visibly drained of colour. "I had nothing to do with it. I knew nothing about it," he blustered.

"I think Mr Hardy you need to think very hard about who was living there and when. I suggest that you really apply you mind to it and not miss anything out."

He started to write. Half an hour later Mandy and Sam had a list of the occupants of the flat in their hands. They made their departure after warning Hardy not to make any more trips abroad in the near future.

Sitting on the train back to Eastbourne, Mandy was studying the names on the list. "We have quite a few here. They will take some tracking down."

"I don't suppose Millicent Nook appears on it?"

"No but I don't think that means much. The place was more or less a flop house and drug den. I am guessing that even the people living there did not know what was going on or who was there half of the time."

"Even if he knew she was shacked up there he wouldn't admit it would he? She was what fourteen, fifteen years old, a minor at the time, " observed Sam before closing his eyes for a good snooze back to Eastbourne.

Chapter 15

"Listen up," said Sam as he called the team together in the incident room. "We have a list of suspects." A fake cheer went up from the assembled.

"John Reynolds , Adrian Bennet, Peter Ward, and Francis Donally are the names that Rod Hardy gave Sam and me when we interviewed him yesterday. So folks we need to track them down and have words with them."

"Lost in Time," said Siskin.

"I doubt that. I am pretty sure you will be able to get their current whereabouts fairly quickly," said Sam.

"No they are a band, Lost in Time."

Mandy said, "would you care to let us in on it, you know for those that are not followers of the music scene?"

"There about the only band from Eastbourne that had some chart success. Listen," he pressed a few buttons on his laptop. The music played.

"Okay I get the drift," said Sam. "Now turn it off."

Potts spoke, "I've googled them. They had three hits and then died. They toured extensively before disbanding about four years ago."

"So we now know who was living at the flat when the baby was murdered."

"What about Millicent Nook? She must have been there at some stage given the fact that the DNA confirms she was the mother," said Merryweather.

"That has to be a fair assumption. It does leave the elephant in the room so to speak as to how she gave birth when she was already deceased?" said Mandy.

"And how do you get round that fact?" said Siskin.

"For the moment is it a problem. However, logically dead people do not give birth, so the obvious conclusion is that Millicent Nook was clearly not dead at that time" said Mandy.

"We have the files now from Midlands and the pathology report. She was clearly identified by her DNA," said Potts.

"Then the DNA must be wrong. Where did they get the comparison sample?"

Potts flicked through the file before answering," her comb."

"Tricky," said Mandy.

"Yes very," said Sam. "There are usually lots of hair in a comb and lots of it will have been viable with the roots. It is likely they would have had a match from a considerable number of samples and so ruling out a stray hair from another source."

"But it could be a stray hair if someone else used the comb," said Merryweather.

Potts spoke up. "There were no other sources of DNA on the comb so you can pretty much knock that theory on the head." He continued, "The DNA was definitely that of Millicent Nook and they compared it to her mum's, Emma. So we have a complete DNA history, grandmother, daughter and granddaughter, the murder victim."

"I need to look at that pathology report myself. Put it on my desk when we finish," said Mandy.

Sam spoke. "If Millicent Nook did not die in the car crash and subsequently gave birth then it is logical to assume that she may still be alive. So put her on the list of people to track down. Once she was pronounced dead they would have ceased the missing person enquiries. All attempts to locate her would have stopped. They thought they had found her in that car near Coventry."

Potts interrupted again. "Good old google I have a hit on Adrian Bennet. There is a news report that he had a stroke and heart attack following a cocaine binge. There was a photo showing him in better times standing beside a Porsche and guess what? It shows the registration number."

"Check the reg with DVLA," said Mandy.

"Already done, he lives local."

Well this is going better than expected," said Sam.

"Everything always goes better than you expect," said Mandy to laughter from the team.

It was a short drive to the small cottage outside of town. It had a drive and a an attached garage. The gravel crushed under Mandy's and Sam's vehicle as they drove onto the driveway. Not the sort of mansion you expect from a rock star," said Sam.

It was small no more than two bedrooms upstairs and two rooms downstairs. It was clear that the property was in need of painting and some maintenance. The garden was wild and untended. It would appear that Mr Adrian Bennet was not the most affluent of individuals.

There was a Volkswagen Lupo on the drive and Sam parked carefully so as not to block it in. He had seen the sign it displayed saying nurse on call. Clearly put there in the hope of avoiding over zealous parking wardens on the streets of Eastbourne.

As they approached the door it opened and a middle aged woman stepped through it. "Oh," she said slightly startled at Mandy and Sam's presence.

"We're here to see Mr Adrian Bennet," said Mandy.

"He doesn't want whatever it is you are selling. So clear off and stop trying to take advantage of him." She was quite fierce and not being a small woman, quite intimidating.

"We are Police Officers," Mandy said in an attempt to placate her. Sam brandished his ID in her line of sight.

"Oh, I am sorry. The word seems to be out that Mr Bennet is unwell and every con man in the area is trying to get him to sign up for everything from a new drive, roofs security alarms to orthopaedic beds, most are overpriced and useless." She gestured them in. "He's through there. She pointed to a door on the left.

"Thank you," said Mandy.

"I have to be off now. Please make sure you close the door properly when you go. He doesn't get many visitors so I imagine he will be pleased to see you." She then shouted out towards the door. "I'll be back to get you to bed later." With that she got in her car and drove off.

Mandy and Sam knocked on the door and entered. The television was on and Adrian Bennet sat in a wheel chair facing it. He looked up as they entered the room. Mandy announced that they were from the Police while he struggled to press the remote to turn the TV off.

"We are here in connection with the disappearance of Millicent Nook. We understand that you shared a flat in Eastbourne with a number of individuals and formed a band called, Lost in Time?" said Mandy.

Adrian uttered a few unintelligible sounds and slowly pointed to his face. It was now clear to Sam and Mandy that he had suffered a severe stroke and that both his speech and movement had been left extremely impaired. They realised that an interview was going to be less than fruitful

Chapter 16

"Yes I was in Lost in Time," replied John Reynolds.

Sam and Mandy had driven to the industrial complex off the M25 motorway adjacent to the Thames River crossing at Dartford. Their drive should have taken just over a hour and a quarter but as usual the traffic had backed up for miles to the tunnel. In the end the time taken was nearly two hours before they turned off.

Reynolds Logistics was sign posted from the roundabout at the turn off, so they had no difficulty in completing the final leg of their journey from Eastbourne. A somewhat annoyed John Reynolds awaited them. They had phoned ahead to make him aware of their intention to interview him. He had rescheduled some meeting or other but their late arrival clearly had put him under time pressure.

"How did you make the leap from rock star to haulier?" asked Sam.

He smiled. "Well it was not that much of a leap more a slow fall. When we started we had a van to lug the gear around, drums, amps, guitars etcetera. We had to hump the gear in and out of the venues ourselves. We couldn't afford roadies or transport. When we got a bit of success the amount of kit we needed for each gig went through the roof. On our European tours we had three articulated lorries that went ahead with the kit for the roadies, stage fitters and sound crew. The cost was unbelievable. At the time it pissed me off. The band were footing the cost and the haulage companies had no idea what they were about,"

"I remember thinking," he continued. "I remember thinking what was needed was a specialist set up that dealt with touring bands, knew what was required, professional and cost effective in what it did."

"So you set up Reynolds Logistic?" said Mandy.

"Well it was not quite as simple as that but eventually, yes. It helped of course that I had been in the business and knew the bands and their management. Word spread and the business grew. Currently we are providing the logistic for six bands on tour across fourteen Countries."

"So you are doing alright financially?" said Sam.

"Well better than I ever did from being in Lost in Time. We hardly made a penny from that, We were ripped off by our manger, the promoters and their so called expenses. At the end of the day we would have made more working in a fast food outlet. It was fun but not profitable."

"Perhaps we could talk about the time before you were famous. We are interested in the time you shared a flat in Eastbourne."

"That was a while ago. There's not much to say about it. It is all a bit hazy."

"Well try and give it a go," said Sam in a voice that indicated to Reynolds that he was not being fobbed off. "Start with who was there?"

He hesitated and feigned a struggle to remember by rubbing his eyes. "Well it was more a flop house really. People came and went all the time drifted in and out. I didn't know half of them."

"I'll make it easy for you. Let's start with you fellow band members shall we? I assume you remember them?" said Mandy.

"Well Adrian and me were in a sort of a band together. I drummed and he rapped over a pre- recorded track. He wrote the lyrics and we sampled the backing. It was just a bit of fun, It was going no-where, I am not sure exactly how we met up with Rod Hardy. He was putting on gigs at local pubs and clubs acting as a promoter. He would book a venue, sell tickets and get people like Adrian and me to play for free. We got a bit of local exposure and he made a few bob."

"Did you know the other members of the band?"

"No, not then that came later. Rod had a knack for collecting people. Look I don't want to admit to anything so before I do on you need to tell me what this is about."

"You know what this is about Mr Reynolds so don't try and play stupid. You like the rest of the Country have seen the news. There was the body of a baby found in the flat you lived in," said Mandy.

"I had nothing to do with that."

"We are just putting the background together. I would suggest that the truth might be the best approach for you at this stage."

He took a moment to consider and then continued. "Rod made a little extra supplying pills and pot."

"In other words he was a drug dealer as well as a music promoter," said Sam.

"Not really a dealer. It was more amongst friends. He real goal was to put a successful band together. He had scouted out a few other likely individuals and introduced us."

"Being Peter Ward and Francis Donally?" said Mandy.

"He rented a flat off of some Greek bloke and set us up in that flat. Francis had a classical training in music. I can't remember where, so she and Adrian started writing songs."

"Okay so the four of you lived there?"

"It wasn't quite like that. Rod also dealt drugs form it. It was used more or less as a drug house. People were there day and night, shooting up and smoking crack."

"And you and the rest of the band?" said Sam.

There was a long pause before he reluctantly replied. "It was available, we were young and we were stupid. We tried it all. We were out of it most of the time."

"What about girls at the flat?"

"There were always girls. They would do almost anything for a fix." he paused. "I am not proud of it but we were young and we took full advantage. It was more or less a continuous sex party, naked girls, drugs booze. We had the drugs and they needed them."

"Putting it another way you and the rest of the band were dealing drugs for Rod Hardy out of the flat and abusing young girls in the process," said Sam.

"No it wasn't like that. We were putting together the music. It just spiralled out of control."

"And Francis?" said Mandy was she part of this?"

"What you think? Just because she was a woman she didn't get into it like the rest of us. She loved it, the drugs, women, men she had the lot. She had no limits."

"Tell us about Millicent Nook."

"I don't know her."

"That is not very clever is it. Lying to us is not a very good idea Mr Reynolds," Sam did his grumpy cop routine without much effort.

There was an awkward silence while Reynolds clearly struggled as to what to say next. Finally he spoke, "There lots of women at the flat. I didn't know their names."

"Nor did you care how old they were. Millicent was fourteen, Mr Reynolds. We know she was at the flat. So think very carefully as to waht you are going to say next."

"There was a young girl but I did not know her age, I think she may have been called Millie. She was only there for a short while. She was

77

wild and I mean wild. She was up for it, with boys and girls."

"And you, did you take full advantage?"

"Look I did not know she was that young."

"For the moment we will leave that. What we want to know is what happened to her?"

"I am not sure. She hung around the band for a while and then dissapeared."

"Do you know if she was pregnant?"

"I know nothing about that. As I said she was out for a good time and the drugs.It was a very confused time."

"Do you know if she ever went to Coventry or Birmigham?" said Mandy.

"It is a possibility, We started touring. Despite all the sex and drugs we did actually put together the rock and roll. We grew a fan base on the internet and by touring. One thing you have to say about Rod Taylor was that, he was a smart guy and knew what he was doing. He got Lost in Time noticed and more to the point started getting us paid and earning money."

" Millicent Nook?" pushed Sam.

"Okay, we kept her around, she was up for it and we all took advantage of it. She was a good looking girl. Who wouldn't?"

"Perhaps someone who was less of a scumbag, Mr Reynolds," said Mandy.

Chapter 17

"Saint Leonards Road, this is it," said Mandy.

"Could do with a lick of paint or something," said Sam as she pulled on the handbrake and turned the engine off.

Inside they sat and waited for twenty minutes. Peter Ward was clearly a busy man. They were in the Eastbourne Social Service's building. Mandy could not help but reflect on the irony of the situation. They were about to interview a man in connection with the murder of a baby and that self same man was now working in the child protection section.

Peter Ward, they discovered had completing his degree and the first part of his training before dropping out and moving to the flat in Eastbourne. Following his time in the band he had returned to complete his training and taken up his current post.

Eventually he appeared and showed them to a small cluttered office. He sat. "The police, would you tell me the case number," he said.

"It is not a child protection issue, Mr Ward," said Sam.

"Oh, I am sorry. I misunderstood. What is it about then?"

"We understand that you were in band called Lost in Time?" said Mandy.

"Well yes that seems like a different time and place now though."

"You as a band all lived together here in Eastbourne before you made it famous?"

"That's right but famous is stretching it. We hit the charts with three songs then sank without a trace. The whole thing lasted about eighteen months then we were back where we started, pot-less and unemployed."

"And you went back to university and finished your course and came here."

"Well that's about it. Although it was a bit more up and down than that," he said.

"We are interested in the period before you were famous when you all lived together. Tell me about it? Who was there?"

"Is this to do with that baby they found on the news?"

Sam nodded, "perhaps you could tell us what you remember and if you can shed some light on it?"

Concern spread across Ward's face. Mandy was less than convinced that he had been unaware of the purpose of their visit. She felt his behaviour fom the moment they had met had been a charade. She knew he had to have been expecting a vist from the police as soon as the body hadd been found and reported on the news, "I was certainly in and out of the flat but I really don't know anything about a baby."

"Well that is not quite how you flat mates remember it. They say you were there most of the time partying and doing drugs."

"I don't admit to substance abuse."

"Of course you don't. That would not do at all given your current position, would it?" said Sam.

"We are not investigating drugs Mr Ward. This is a murder enquiry so I would suggest that you try and be a little more frank," said Mandy. "Shall we try again. Tell me about your time there?"

"Okay, I was out of it. It is not a period of my life I am proud of. I lost it completely. I was addicted to herion, coke, meth. You name it, I was doing it. The fact that Lost in Time bombed after a year and a bit was the best thing that could have happend to me. I was broke and out of it. It is a haze . I was sectioned under the Mantal Health Act and it saved my life. I got into rehab and got clean. As you can see I eventually got my life back on track. It helps me to understand the young people I deal with here on a day to day basis. So some good came of it all."

"You do not deny being at the flat when the death occurred?" said Sam.

"I don't know anything about a baby."

"Tell about Millicent Nook," pushed Mandy.

"Who?"

"Don't try that or I'll have you out of here in handcuffs and down the Nick in front of everyone," said Sam at his grumpyist.

Ward swallowed visible and the colour drained from his face. "The young girl, Millie, I never touched her."

"You need to stop lying to us, perverting the course of justice is a real offense. So think before you open you mouth and say something else you may regret."

"I did not know her age.."

"At this stage we are not looking at anything other than murder," soothed Mandy.

"It was just how it was. She and Francis partied hardy. They had no limits."

"And you and the rest of the band took full advantage."

"Not just us they both turned tricks to earn money to get drugs. They were always having sex with someone. As I said it was out of control. It was party time all the time."

"How come you managed to make music?"

"It is a questionI ask myself. Somehow Rod held us together. Somehow he turned our lifestyle into a positive. Ninety per cent of music is hype and PR. Rod was good at both. That is not to say we did not have some talent. We wrote songs and we could play. You know the saying that you can't polish a turd well Rod could. Well at least long enough for him to make a fortune before he ditched us and we distintigrated."

"Who got Millicent Nook pregnant?" said Mandy.

"I did not know," he paused as the sentance sunk in."The baby, it was hers?"

"We belive so. Now tell us how it came to be murdered and hiden in the wall of the flat."

"I did not know she was pregnant, honestly. I know nothing about a baby."

"You can understand that given the fact that you all lived together and were having regular sex with her that we find it hard to beleive that you were unaware that she was pregnant?"

"It sounds bad but it is the truth."

"It is unbelievable," said Sam.

They were back at the station and sat in Mandy's office. "What do you think?" said Sam.

"I think they all knew what happened but that's a far cry from proving anything."

"So far we have spoken to Rod Hardy and he seems the sort of individual that has little regard for anything or anyone but himself. Adrian Bennett won't be a lot of help sat in his wheelchair and Peter Ward certainly is not going to say anything if he can help it"

"John Reynolds was not much help either," said Mandy.

"That only leaves Francis Donally to track down and interview. We know she can't have been the father but she could have been a murderer."

"You seem to be missing the obvious suspect, Millicent Nook. That last thing in the World she wanted or needed was a kid in her life."

"There is still the problem that she was dead before she had the baby. We need to get to the bottom of that first," said Sam.

"Well I have had a chance to look at the file on her death in the car crash."

"You know what happened don't you."

"I think I do," said Mandy.

Chapter 18

"Round up time," said Mandy as they gathered in the incident room,

"So far we are getting nowhere fast," said Sam. "We have interviewed Emma Nook, the deceased baby's Grandmother. She appears to know nothing about the baby and as far as as we can tell believes her daughter Millicent to have died in a car crash."

"Adrian Bennett's life style seems to have caught up with him and he is in a wheelchair having suffered a massive stroke, presumably after overdoing on cocaine and whatever else," said Mandy.

"Rod Hardy is a slimy as a bag off gone of fish and just as unsavoury. He admits to renting the flat, here In Eastbourne but denies knowing anything else."

"Peter Ward seems to have moved on and now works, here in Eastbourne, in Social Services. Like the rest he can't remember and knows nothing."

"John Reynolds has fallen on his feet and runs a logistics business moving bands and their kit around on tour."

"Which leaves us with Francis Donally?" said Potts.

"And Millicent," said Mandy.

Merryweather spoke. "What I cannot understand if Millicent did not die in the car crash, carried on living at the flat and then gave birth then surely the rest of them would be able to confirm it."

"That's the conundrum. Basically they claim not to remember when she arrived and when she left. They all claim not to know of a baby," said Mandy.

"That leaves two possibilities. One, she left and died in a car crash and they know nothing. Two.." said Siskin.

"They are all lying. She never died. She was at the flat, gave birth, the baby was murdered and the body hidden." said Potts.

"My money is on number two. There is no doubt that she was not killed in the car crash and was there when she had a baby. Anyone of the male members living there could have been the father or any number of other men who frequented the flat. It is pretty obvious that Millicent and Frances were making money selling their bodies. Not one of them had a job. Rod Hardy may have been letting them live there rent free but he does not strike me as stupid enough to be giving them bundles of cash to to party and do drugs. They were living off of the two girls."

"It is all pretty sordid, especially when you consider Millicent was still a school girl," said Potts.

"That pretty sums the character of the people we are dealing with, sordid," said Mandy. "There were living a hedonistic existence without any regard for anyone or anything."

"So given their attitude and manner of living, we cannot rule out any of them as suspects. They were a bunch of low life's, out for themselves," said Sam.

"So who do we have as our prime suspect?" said Siskin , looking to Mandy.

" Millicent," said Mandy. "She had to be there. The question is did she actually murder her own baby? We need to find out what exactly happened."

Siskin said," we need to find out, how a dead person gives birth first."

"Oh I know that," said Mandy.

"Perhaps you would like to tell us," said Sam.

"It is in the pathologists report. You just needed to read it."

"Right, how about you just tell us and cut the suspense," said Sam.

"The facts are that the Fire Service and the Police are called out, by a passing motorist on his way to work, to a car that has burnt out in a field. They find a charred body in the vehicle. Whoever else was in that car was long gone. I believe there were at last two other people in it apart from the deceased."

"How can you know that?" said Merryweather.

"I cannot know for certain but I am fairly confident. Now when I get in a car as a passenger and say Sam is driving, I get in the front alongside him. The body was in the back suggesting the front passenger seat was occupied."

"How does that help?" said Potts.

"It helps in the fact that we know that Millicent could not drive. So if she was there had to be a someone driving. They had to be at least a total of three people in that stolen car. The driver, the deceased and Millicent."

"Why would she have to be in the car?" said Merryweather.

"Because she had to have been at the scene for what occurred to have happened," She said.

"So what did happen?" said Siskin.

"As I said I cannot be one hundred per cent but here is what I think." She paused.

"You are milking this, get on with it," said Sam.

"Millicent was in Birmingham or somewhere in the Midlands the previous night. I have an idea why but it will need to be checked out. Anyway she is there. At some stage she and at least two others steal a car and go for a joy ride."

"There was her and another girls in the car, the driver and possibly more occupants. High on drink or drugs they play at formulae one. The driver loses control and they crash. They all get out relatively uninjured apart from one."

"They are dazed, under the influence and stumbling about in the pitch black. At some stage they realise that the girl is dead. They are in deep trouble. This had gone from a case of taking and driving to manslaughter, while under the influence of drink or drugs."

"What to do?" continued Mandy. "Whatever the discussion they come to the conclusion to torch the car with the body it it. There was petrol everywhere in the car. Remember the tank ruptured in the crash."

"That way they had a good chance that any finger print or DNA evidence would go up in flames with the car." said Potts.

"So we have the group, including Millicent stood in a field, in the middle of nowhere and a burning car with a body in it. They need to get away from the scene. They are miles away from anywhere. We know they did not walk anywhere or call a taxi. The Police investigation was extensive and they found nothing. My guess is they they phoned someone to get them"

"Did the investigation turn up any mobile phone pings in the area?" said Siskin.

"Yes but they do not have an exact time for the call. The car was found hours after. There were hundred of calls in the area. They can't track them all and remember back then you could just buy a phone, with a number and top it up with a voucher that you could buy anywhere for cash. Most kids used them as no bank account was needed." said Mandy.

"So they phone a friend,et picked up and disappear," said Sam.

"Right, except they leave something behind and this is where it all gets turned upside-down. The police recover a comb at the scene. Now you have to go back a few years. DNA was not as developed. You needed a good viable sample, the test was harder to do, you needed a complete sample. All these things played into what happened next."

"The forensic team label the comb as found on the victim. It is a tiny difference but crucial. It was lying in the field near the front of the car. I am guessing it fell from Millicent's pocket or bag when she stumbled out."

"No one checks it, no one questions how it could have survived when the owner is so badly burnt. I have checked the log. Uniform were there first. Then the forensics who scoured the area and car. The Detectives turned up hours later and find little to see."

"A week or even months later the DNA results come in. They assume the sample was from the body. It would not have made much difference in any event. It was the only clue they had to the deceased. Their enquiries turned up nothing else." said Mandy.

"Let me guess they run it through the system and get a match to Millicent," said Sam.

"She had been reported missing. The Police here in Eastbourne had attended her house, taken samples, from her belongings and her Mother. They are in doubt they have their car crash victim," said Mandy.

"They never identified who was in the car with her?" said Siskin.

"No," said Mandy. "Millicent is officially dead. Now this is where it gets a whole lot worst for us."

"How so?" said Merryweather.

"Let's follow it through. If she isn't the deceased there must be the real victim out there. A young girls has disappeared without a trace.

Some parent is out there, waiting for their daughter, who went on a night out and never came back. We need to find out who that girl was."

"We now know that Millicent is alive. Where is she? She is the prime suspect in our murder."

Chapter 19

Superintendent Taylor had driven to Eastbourne from Brighton where he was based. He looked harassed and irritable as he walked into Mandy's office without knocking. She startled slightly at his sudden appearance. "I wasn't expecting you, Sir," she said as she got up from behind her desk.

"As you were," she resumed her position on her chair as he sat in the one on the opposite side of the desk. He placed his hat on the desk. It was wet. She deduced from that it was still raining a fact she could have easily determined by looking out of the window. She moved her files away from his hat noting that the corners were slightly soggy from the run off.

"The baby murder?" He sat and waited.

"The DNA evidence was flawed and we now believe that Millicent was alive as was the mother. In truth that was something we knew from the start. Dead women do not give birth months after they are buried."

"Quite so," he was interrupted as Potts walked in with two cups of coffee. Mandy was surprised by this. It had been her turn to make the coffee and she had been putting it off despite glaring glances from her colleagues in the incident room she could see through her office window. He winked as he put the cups down.

As he was leaving Sam appeared in the doorway. "Any chance?" he said referring to the coffee. Mandy saw Potts mouth, "up yours" before departing and allowing Sam to pass.

"Morning Sergeant," said Taylor.

"Sir," Sam acknowledged the greeting before taking his seat at the desk alongside the Superintendent.

Mandy continued her update. "Our first task is to determine if Millicent is still alive and track her down."

"What about the earlier investigation when she was first reported missing by her Mother?"

"It just stopped and the file was closed. As far as the investigating officers were concerned she had turned up dead in a RTC and there was no point therefore in looking to trace her further. No one was looking for her. We are looking now, though"

"Even if she had been arrested and DNA taken it would be unlikely that they would have identified her. Who would think to run a check against a deceased road traffic victim?" said Sam.

"Having said that, we have run her DNA and name through the data basis and nothing has turned up as yet. She went completely off the radar after her supposed death." said Mandy.

"She has never been arrested where a DNA sample was taken. That has been checked."We are currently waiting for results from employment records. We assume she is earning a living somewhere and must have applied for a National Insurance Number."

"Well that should be a relatively easy way to find her," commented Taylor.

"You would have thought so wouldn't you?" said Sam. "Sadly not though, it turns out the Department of Works and Pensions was outsourced year's ago. It is quite easy to end up with a new NI number by a slip of your employers pen. There was no checking process when an employer set up a record. So if the wages clerk just reversed a number when your details were sent to the Employment Department a new record was created for tax and another for national insurance. Apparently there are thousands of us that have been contributing under the wrong NI number. It is usually spotted when you come up to retirement age. You find that a load of the contributions that you have made are missing and your pension had been reduced. The pensioner obviously queries it and they go looking and find them under a different NI number."

"What happens if the pensioner just accepts it."

"Saves the Country money on its Old Age Pension Bill," said Sam.

"Just another complication but the point is no one looked for her so she could have just been declared dead then just got a job the next day or walked in to a doctors or hospital for treatment."

"Hospitals, she did have a baby after all?" said Taylor.

"Nothing she certainly did not give birth in one," said Mandy.

"And there is no record of her registering with a doctor."

"So she is assumed dead and for all intents and purposes she disappears from the face of the Earth. Do you think she was murdered after she gave birth. As far as the World was concerned she was already dead, after all?" said Taylor.

Mandy thought for a moment. "I don't think so. I obviously cannot be sure but I think not. The most likely suspects would be the members of the band, Lost in Time. They were a group of idiots and junkies. I am sure they know more. They are all lying about Millicent and obscuring the facts. My instinct is they know what happened to the baby but to murder Millicent and dispose of her body is another matter. I don't think they were capable."

"The pressing thing and the reason I have popped in is the girl burnt to death in the car," said Taylor.

"I am assuming that the Birmingham coppers are not over the moon at having to re-open the case?"

"Well it was never officially closed and they are still looking for the other occupants, of course. Your reasoning in that the body was not Millicent's is sound but as far as they are concerned the have a DNA match to the deceased," said Taylor.

"But it can't be her logically. She gave birth after," said Sam.

"They would prefer to see it as us somehow muddling our DNA. That is to say we have it wrong and Millicent is not the mother."

"It's the cost," said Mandy.

"Look at it this way. We have to exhume a body, That is not going to be a very nice thing for her Mother. What's her name, Emma? What if you are wrong, have you thought of that?"

"I am not wrong," said Mandy emphatically.

"Okay, then Birmingham have to start the investigation from scratch and find out who this girl was," said Taylor.

"It is cost," repeated Mandy.

Taylor looked slightly annoyed. "Budgets are tight but I agree that it should not be the driving force. However we need to be one hundred per cent sure that the body is the graveyard here in Eastbourne is not that of Millicent Nook before we go stumbling in. It may be a complete waste of time. We could exhume the body and they might not even be able to get a viable sample of DNA, It was badly burnt and had been in the ground for years."

"I know there is only a small chance of identifying the victim but we have to try don't we? You have children. Just imagine one of them went out for an evening and just disappeared and was never heard of again? You would want the Police to get answers whatever the cost," said Mandy.

Taylor sat quietly for a moment. "You are right of course. These cuts make the decisions so hard. Money spent in one place means that it isn't available elsewhere. There isn't enough to do this job properly. We all signed up to the job to catch the bad guys but we know that we are just not able to do it properly."

"So," said Sam.

"I'll start the process and let's hope we can give some missing girls Mother a little peace of mind and comfort."

Chapter 20

Adrian Bennett sat watching the television. His nurse had helped him wash and get into his night clothes. She had left a few minutes previously. The Agency had failed to send the daily help and he had spent a miserable day struggling to get to the toilet and prepare food.

He had exaggerated the extent of his paralysis when Mandy and Sam had interviewed him. His speech was bad but slowly improving and there was more movement in his left side, not enough to fend for himself but enough to lift a spoon and struggle from wheelchair to bed.

He knew they would be back and he would not be able to avoid their questions indefinitely. He had thought the whole thing was over. It was years ago and so much water was under the bridge. The Band had gone from living a life of squalor in a clapped out flat in Eastbourne to World tours in five star luxury hotels and stretched limos.

They had it made or so he thought, women, drugs, booze money and fame. Little did he realise that he would all pass so quickly. How fleeting it would all be. It seemed it had been no more than an instant when they had been number one and then consigned to yesterday's news.

The money had disappeared. He knew that the stadiums they filled with concert goers grossed millions of pounds. Lost in Time saw a few pounds of it. The rest just seem to evaporate. Rod Hardy though did alright. He had a lawyer look at it. The result was not promising. He could sue, try and recover some of the money but it would cost. Lawyers are not cheap and wanted to be sure they would get paid. It was far from certain where the money had gone and if he would win his case. He did not have the money to pay the legal fees.

He had managed to earn some money from reality television appearances, just enough to buy the house he now lived in. It was the only sensible thing he ever did. The television work dried up and his funds diminished. He just could not let the fame go. He wanted that feeling again, the fans the rush, the buzz.

They were always there like vultures picking at a corpse, the hangers on. They told him what he wanted to hear, that he could be famous again, number one. He had never broken his drug habit and that did not help the cause of rational decision making.

He went back in the recording studio. He would carve out a career as a solo artist. Why not many had done so before him? His entourage encouraged him, told him he was brilliant and he could not fail. He believed it. They record companies did not.

He paid for the recording studio. He paid the producers. He paid the engineers and he paid the musicians. His so called friends were with him every step of the way and he was paying for them to have a continuous party.

It was a disaster. The A&R men at the record companies listened to the recording politely and just as politely never called him back. He tried to promote himself, more money down the drain. His friends disappeared as the money ran out. His drug use escalated.

He could not remember the night he had the stroke. In fact by then he could remember very little about anything. His life was fully centred on the next fix. He woke up in hospital paralysed and unable to speak. He was recovering but he knew that he would never do so fully. He also knew that the past was catching up with them all. The police were knocking on doors and wanted answers. The secret had been kept so far. He doubted that it would remain that way.

He had debated if he should talk to the police. He might be able to cut a deal. Turn Queen's evidence or whatever it was that gave you immunity from prosecution. Mandy and Sam had left without answers once. He knew they would be back. He had a solicitor coming in two days and would discuss it with him.

He was not sure how he felt about the events in that flat on the day the baby was killed. Through the haze of drugs and drink it had seemed no big deal. It had not even seemed real. Now clean not by choice but by circumstances it felt differently. Sitting here alone struggling to move and talk life had taken on a different meaning. Time and circumstances had a way of doing that.

Adrian Bennet was in danger of doing the right thing for once. It even surprised him that he felt this way. He knew his fellow band members may not see it in the same light but he really did not care. They continued on with their lives. They had not even been bothered to visit him, no bunch or grapes when his was in hospital, not even a get well card. He owed them exactly what they had given him, nothing.

His thoughts were interrupted by what he took to be the sound of car tyres on gravel. He assumed the nurse had returned. He heard the car door slam and the front door open. He expected the door to the lounge where he and his bed had been moved to open. It did not. Sounds of drawers opening in the small kitchen next door could be heard as he used the remote to turn the volume lower on the television.

The door opened and the figure entered carrying a large kitchen knife.

The next morning with Mandy driving, she and Sam reached Adrian Bennet's home and parked on the road. The police tapes were up protecting the crime scene and the unformed officers were awaiting their arrival. The Volkswagen Lupo they saw on their last visit was parked on the gravel drive.

They were approached the Crime Scene Officer as they walked towards the house. "The deceased in one Adrian Bennet, the house owner. His throat was cut sometime yesterday evening. His nurse discovered him when she called in on her daily visit."

"Thank you officer," said Sam.

"Take a statement from the nurse," said Mandy.

They entered the lounge after putting covers on their shoes and pulling on latex gloves. Lab technicians dressed in white overalls were video taping, photographing and swabbing the scene. "Jesus, I never get used to this," said Sam.

Mandy had to admit the sight before them was pretty gruesome. There was blood everywhere and Adrian Bennett's head had almost been severed from his neck. He had not die immediately and blood had pumped from the wound and arterial spray had covered the scene .

They were approached by the lead forensic investigator. "What can you tell us so far?" Mandy said.

"Well as you see someone cut his throat and made a lot of mess. The knife was next to the body." he held up a plastic bag in which there was a large carving knife. "It matches the set in the kitchen"

"So the killer did not bring their own weapon?"

"Well we can't be one hundred per cent until we test it but I would say so. He or she took the knife from the kitchen and used it on the victim."

"Time?" said Sam.

""We took the liver temperature and he had been dead since early yesterday evening."

"It looks a fairly violent attack, personal," said Mandy.

"I don't know. There was just one cut, not multiple stab wounds as you would get if it were a more passionate attack fuelled by anger. It looks messy because of the quantity of blood but it was clinical and efficient."

"Put him out of his misery, so to speak?" said Sam.

"Or someone who did not care one way of the other, more like clearing up the rubbish," said Mandy.

"Means of entry?"

"The door was left on the latch," by the nurse. "Apparently she had a number of visits to do in a day and fiddling around with keys is a pain."

"Great so anyone can just wander in"

"Do you think it is connected to Millicent and the baby?" said Sam when they were in the car.

"Coincidences like murder don't figure high on my list of everyday things that just happen. Someone is cleaning up any witnesses to the events at the flat"

Chapter 21

"Do you think we will get time to do some Christmas Shopping?" said Siskin.

"It depends how long it takes to interview this Rod Hardy bloke," said Merryweather. They were walking from the train station to the underground at Victoria, having caught the six fifty train from Eastbourne, which turned into the six fifty nine, which then became delayed and arrived just over an hour late.

"I was thinking we could go to Hamleys," said Siskin.

"Probably the best toy shop in the World," said Merryweather mimicking the voice over of a television lager advertisement. ""You don't have kids, do you?"

"Well no, I have a nephew."

"No you don't. You are an only child."

Siskin was silent briefly. "It is coming up to Christmas and they do really good stuff."

"That's lame," said Merryweather. "But you are right. It is brilliant there. It depends on how long it takes with our suspect but I wouldn't mind going and I do have children."

It took longer than they had expected. They were informed that Rod

Hardy had a breakfast meeting with a client that he could not defer. They sat in the small anti room to his office for another hour. It was twelve fifteen by the time Hardy appeared at his office. The two detectives had been up and on duty since six that morning and now six hours later they were about to finally speak to a suspect in Adrian Bennet's murder.

Sitting in Rod Hardy's office, Siskin was finally able to put the question, "where were you two nights ago, between six and midnight?"

Now given that he was only asking what Hardy had been doing day ago he expected an immediate answer. After all no great feat of memory was required. Instead Hardy opened up his lap top and began tapping keys. "Let me see. I will need to check my diary," he said.

Siskin knew that he was just trying to annoy them. It did give them an insight into the type of man he was though. Siskin read two things into his pedantic behaviour. Firstly, he like the element of control, he had the power to make them wait and he was using it. Secondly, he thought himself superior to them. He had a big ego and liked to demonstrate how good he was.

"Here it is," he finally decided to answer what was a very simple question. I went home to change at four thirty and then attended a dinner at the Cafe Royale at seven thirty I left at about one thirty a.m."

"I assume someone saw you there?" said Merryweather.

"About two hundred people."

"Just a few names will do."

"I am sure my secretary will give you a guest list. Why do you want to know?"

"Adrian Bennet was murdered, His body was discovered at his home yesterday morning," said Siskin.

Standing on the pavement outside his office, holding a list of witness Merryweather spoke first. "Total arsehole."

"Succinct but lacks a certain amount of true analysis. He may not have had the opportunity to kill Bennet but I have little doubt he is a grade A narcissist and would not think twice about killing a baby if it was getting in his way. Or as you put it, a total arsehole."

"We could check his alibi at the Cafe Royale though."

"Doesn't seem much point," said Siskin.

"Okay if you say so but it is very close to Hamleys."

****

Mandy sat opposite Peter Ward in the Eastbourne Social Service's building. "I am sorry to have to tell you that Adrian Bennet was found yesterday. He had been murdered the previous evening."

He looked taken aback at the news but not greatly shocked. "And you want to know where I was?"

"That's about it. Where were you?"

"Where I always am, at home with my wife."

"She can vouch for this?" said Mandy.

"We have just had a baby son, three months ago. I go straight home as soon as I finish up. I like to be there for bath time."

"Were you out visiting clients, so to speak. prior to that?"

"Yes, I think my last visit was at four thirty. I timed it to be there when they returned from the school run."

"So there is the possibility then that you could have driven to Mr Bennet's house on your way home," she stated.

"But I didn't."

"What car do you drive?"

"A Volkswagen Polo," he said.

"Did you know where Mr Bennet lived?"

"Yes I visited once or twice, but it was a waste of time. I tried to persuade him to get help with his drink and drug addiction but he was not interested, In the end I gave up and carried on with my life. It came as no surprised he was dead but murdered? Are you sure?"

She did not bother to answer that. She would get one of her team to interview his wife to corroborate his story later.

***

Sam. this time accompanied by Potts, had a repeat of the drive to the industrial estate adjacent to Queen Elisabeth II crossing that he had with Mandy. Fed up with the traffic they eventually drove into Reynold's Logistic's haulage yard.

They eventually managed to find Reynolds in the yard in conversation with some drivers. He saw them and recognising Sam stopped and made his way to them. "Didn't expect to see you so soon," he said.

"Something's happened and we need to know where you were two evenings ago?"

"I was in Manchester driving an artic"

"Artic?"said Potts.

Reynolds looked at him as though he was soft in the head. Sam answered for him, " articulated lorry."

"A semi," said Potts.

"Too much American television," said Reynolds and Sam was forced to agree.

"I thought you ran the Company?" said Sam.

"So did I but we have a few bands on tour and one of the drivers went walk about. I can't afford to leave people stranded. It would kill my reputation. So I had to step in and take up the slack. Why are you asking?"

"Adrian Bennet's been murdered," said Potts.

There was a moment's silence while Reynolds absorbed the information. "About time somebody killed the shit."

"I gather from that he wasn't your favourite person?" said Sam.

"He was a waste of space, a junkie. The rest of us made an effort to at least get on stage in a fit state to play. He did not give a hoot. All he did was party and screw up the performances. He more than anybody led to the collapse of Lost in Time. Then he tried suing the rest of us claiming he had written the songs. He hadn't of course Francis Donally did most of them. But in is addled brain he was the victim and had been short changed."

"Was there any truth in his claims?"

"Like bollocks, we were all ripped off by Rod Hardy our so called manager. The only thing he managed to do was keep all the money for himself, Now he's someone I would like to see murdered. Adrian was just a waste of space, greedy but stupid. Hardy on the other hand is a grade one piece of crap."

"Well," said Potts as they began the drive back. "That is a very angry man."

"But not the man, on the face of it that killed Mr Bennet."

Chapter 22

Mandy was dreading what Sam and she had to do next. They sat in silence as Sam drove them to Emma Nook's house. For once even Sam was not moaning about anything but concentrated on driving. They arrived at her road to find there was nowhere to park outside. Even though they were forced to park halfway down the street, Sam still resisted the urge to grumble as they walked to her door.

The door opened as they made their way up the path. They had telephoned ahead to ensure that she would be there. She had obviously keep watch on their car and seen their arrival. "Come in," she said.

They followed her into the living room. Mandy and Sam sat side by side on the sofa facing her. There was an awkward silence as Mandy struggle to find a way to open the conversation. Emma detected the unease emanating from her and lent forward. "What is it?" she said.

Mandy took a deep breath and started from the beginning. There was no easy way of saying what she had to tell her. "You may have seen from the newspapers and the television coverage that a baby's body was discovered in a flat in Eastbourne?"

"Of course, it is awful."

"On our last visit I said we were re-examining the circumstances of Millicent's death. I was less than frank. I did not tell you why we were doing so."

Emma made no reaction. She sat waiting for Mandy to continue.

"We have reason to believe that Millicent was not killed in the car crash." She waited for Emma to digest what she had just told her. There was still little reaction other than a look of concentration. She finally spoke. "I don't understand," was all she said.

"You don't seemed surprised," said Sam.

She paused before replying. " I never believed she was dead. I just felt it inside."

"I see," said Mandy. "I need to ask you this again. Have you heard from her since the crash."

"No, nothing."

Sam seeing that Mandy was struggling intervened. "The reason we believe she may have not been the victim in the car crash is that the baby found in the flat was hers. That baby was born after her supposed death." He stopped talking letting his words sink in.

"In other words?" Emma remained calm taking it in.

"In other words Mrs Nook, I have no way of saying this in a way any Mother would want to her but I can only tell you what we understand. Your daughter did not die, She gave birth to a baby girl and that child was subsequently murdered."

Emma sat white faced and uttered a small gasp. "I have a grand daughter?". Then she realised the awful truth. The strength drained from her and she seemed to visibly shrink into the chair. "I see," was all she said.

"I am sorry to have to tell you this," said Mandy. "I am afraid there is more."

"Where is Millicent now?"

"We don't know, I am afraid. We are looking for her?"

Mandy continued, "as I said there is more. You need to understand that if Millicent was not killed in the car crash then we need to find out who was."

Emma was looking bewildered. "I don't understand any of this. What are you saying?"

Mandy tried to convey her message as sympathetically as she could. "We need to find out who the girl was that died? We need to exhume the body and try and extract DNA. Somewhere there are parents out there still morning for their missing daughter. We need to find out who this girl is?"

"You want to dig Millicent up?" said Emma horrified.

Mandy realised that Emma was not coping with the situation. Her brain was not processing the information. This woman in a matter of moments had to process the fact that her daughter, she thought dead for seven years may be alive, that she had a granddaughter that had been murdered and that the police were now exhuming the body.

"We do not believe it is Millicent."

"I see," she said. "I think I need you to go now." She stood up. She said no more and showed them out.

Mandy and Sam sat in the car. "That was odd," said Mandy as Sam started the engine.

"What was odd?"

"Her reaction I suppose."

"I am not sure what my reaction would be if someone told me a child of mine, I though dead wasn't. I had a grand child I knew nothing and that she had been murdered. I am not sure anything in life prepares you for that, do you?"

"I understand all that but there was something. I don't know what though."

They sat in silence as they drove back to the police station. The team was busy at work as they walked through the Incident room to Mandy's office. She sat quietly ordering the recent events in her mind.

She was now confronted with two murders, the baby and Adrian Bennett. The obvious assumption was that Bennet had been murdered to cover up the first murder.

They had traced all the Lost in Time band members and their manager Rod Hardy, except Francis Donally. The main suspect in the murder of the infant had to be her mother Millicent. The girl burnt in the car crash, she felt would be identified fairly quickly if they managed to extract DNA from the exhumation process. The key to it all was to track down Millicent and interview her.

She left her office and called the team to order. "We need to prioritise the following."

"One, find Millicent Nook. She is out there somewhere so find her."

"Two, track down Francis Donally the last member of Lost in Time."

"Three, there must be a connection between the girl that died in the car crash and Millicent. Find out how her DNA was at the scene."

"Four, there must have been at least one other person, the driver at the crash, so find out how he and Millicent left the scene. Someone else knows what happened that night because they drove to the crash, picked Millicent and the driver up."

She called Sam over. "I know what was bothering me when we were interviewing Emma Nook."

"Go on," he urged. He knew from past experience that she picked up on the tiniest detail and those details could often make or break the case.

"Emma Nook did not ask the obvious question, did she?" Sam looked puzzled. Mandy continued. "She never asked where Millicent was or if she was still alive? But there is something else niggling at the back of my mind as well. I know it was when we were walking to her house from where we had to park so far away but I just can't put my finger on it. It will come to you, it always does."

Chapter 23

"How's the thinking going?" said Sam as he wondered into Mandy's office, eating his morning bacon butty and holding a coffee. He placed the cup on her desk adding to the the cup rings already present and took a seat. He put his bacon roll down as he retrieved the file he had tucked under his arm.

"We could save a lot of money on cleaners. There seems little point in them coming in overnight, dusting and vacuum cleaning when you are going to come in first thing in the morning and throw crumbs and coffee everywhere."

Sam looked at the crumbs on her desk and lent froward and swept them onto the floor. "Well that's sorted then," said Mandy sarcastically. He ignored her, pick up the butty and took another bite. This time a dribble of ketchup ended up on his chin.

She gave up as she watched and waited for that to to end up on either her desk or the floor. "To answer your question I have been thinking. Is that the interview statements taken from the witnesses at Adrian Bennet's?"

He pushed the file across. She began to read through. He sat quietly eating and then finished off his breakfast with a big swig of coffee. Mouth finally empty he spoke,"anything?"

"Here it is. The car the nurse drives, a Volkswagen and the neighbour saw it leaving at around eight o'clock."

"So, she goes every evening. That's not suspicious."

"You are making the same mistake as the Officer that interviewed the neighbour. The nurse said she left much earlier so what he thought was her car couldn't have been. We have our first lead."

Sam picked up the file and started to read. "I'll get uniform to nip back and re-interview the neighbour and see if we can get more on the car. I run a DVLA check and see if any of our suspects own a Volkswagen."

"You can start with Peter Ward. When I interviewed him he said he drove a Volkswagen something. I know that the nurse drives a Lupo but the neighbour could be mistaken. Golfs, Polos and Lupos all look similar. In any event find out the colour and see if we can drill down on the model."

"I'll get that started," he said getting up. Mandy watched as more crumbs tumbled from his lap in the process.

She sat back in her chair and stared into the middle distance. There was something else. It was there at the back of her mind. Something to do with the car. She knew she had seen a Volkswagen somewhere but she could not picture it in her mind. It was like trying to remember the answer to a quiz question. It was on the tip of her tongue but it just wouldn't come out. She knew it would come but it was just frustrating waiting for it.

Siskin walked in. She had not heard him knock, wrapped up in her own thoughts as she was. She started slightly at his appearance. "Sorry, I was miles away. What is it?"

"Can I sit?" She gestured for him to do so. "Lost in Time, I have been digging back through there history, tour dates, gigs and the like. I think I have something. I printed this off the internet." He passed the sheet of paper to her.

She picked it up and began to read. It was in the form of a flyer advertising the band's appearance at a pub. The first thing she noted was the date. It was the night of the fatal car crash when a girl was burnt to death. "Where is the Lady Godiva?" she said.

"Coventry, it was a large pub with a hall attached. They used to put on live bands once or twice a week."

"So we can place all our suspects ten or twelve miles from the scene of the car crash?"

"A bit more than that. The car that that was stolen was parked two roads away. On the next corner is a Kebab takeaway. I am guessing it did a roaring trade after the Lady Godiva turned out. It stayed open until three in the morning whenever there was a gig."

"So it would be reasonable to assume that having played our band went in the search of food?"

"That's what I think happened. They had a few drinks by then, headed for a Kebab and saw the car. We can't say who was involved but at least a couple of them decided it was a good idea to take a joy ride."

"Well we know that Millicent was one of them. We should assume that the other female passenger was at the pub and watched the band perform. She was probably picked up by one of the band members and got in the car for a laugh."

"There it gets more difficult. The pub has been shut for years. It was pay at the door so we have no idea who was at the performance that night. There is no CCTV. It does not get us much further, I am afraid," said Siskin.

"It will get the Coventry Police pointing in the right direction. They at least know for certain they are looking for a young female that went missing around that time and that she would be relatively local to the Lady Godiva. I am guessing back then people did not travel from miles around to watch a little know band like Lost in Time."

"If they manage to extract DNA from the body then we shall be able to give them a lot more. They are exhuming her at the moment. I have asked them to fast track the testing, so if they recover anything we will know by close of play tomorrow."

Mandy said nothing about Siskin's enthusiasm for getting a quick DNA result. She felt that Superintendent Taylor would have been less inclined to spend the money of getting it processed immediately to help another Police Force.

She brushed the remaining crumbs off her desk before making her way through to the incident room. She clapped her hands to get the teams attention.

"We now have two murders to solve, Millicent Nook's baby and Adrian Bennet. We also have two suspects we haven't found yet, Millicent herself and Francis Donally. Find them. I am sure that Sam has you looking at the cars they all drive, but don't just concentrate on their cars. We need to know what cars they have access to. Check the cars of their spouses, kids, employers and close family. If I were off to murder Bennet I probably would not chose to nip off and do it in my own car. If we can get a registration number then we can start on CCTV and number plate recognition. If we have a car the chances are we will be able to track its movements.

"We know that the night of Millicent's supposed death the band, Lost in Time had a performance close by. We can't know which band members took the car that crashed but we can be sure that she and an unknown local girl were in it. My best guess is that after the crash they phoned someone in the band to come and pick them up from the crash site. So there are two lines of enquiry to follow up on, phone records and the van used to transport the band around at that time. Go back over the earlier investigation. We now have the advantage of knowing who we are looking for."

"Now we know that Millicent was not killed in the car crash she has to be our chief suspect in the murder of her baby," said Sam. "We know she did not did not do it alone. Someone and likely more than one person had to have been involved. The plastering of bodies behind walls was not part of Millicent's skill set. The people living in that flat had at least to have been aware of the murder. Treat all of Lost in Time and Rod Hardy, their manager as murder suspects."

"We have to assume at this stage that Adrian Bennet was killed because he was about to come clean. We need to find out if he had been in contact with the other members of the band, or Hardy and Millicent. We know that Peter Ward kept in touch with Bennet. He has an alibi but double check it and check all their phone records. See who was in contact with whom. The quicker we find Millicent and Francis the quicker we will get to the bottom of it."

Merryweather interrupted. "I think I have found Francis Donally."

Chapter 24

There was a moments silence in the Incident Room at the announcement that the last member of Lost in Time, Francis Donally had been found. "Well don't keep it to yourself. Where is she and how did you track her down?" said Sam.

Merryweather took the floor. "We knew the band toured abroad a lot so I went back to the press coverage. I started around the time they broke up. It was fairly simple really from there. They played their last gig in Athens. It was a shambles. The drink and drugs had taken over and the critics panned it. Lost in Time disintegrated live on stage."

"Armed with the fact that the last place they were, was in Greece," he continued. " I made enquiries with the Athens's Police. I have to admit they are not the quickest in dealing with matters. This was over a week ago and I have only just received a response. She was on the Island of Crete."

"Was?" said Mandy. "Where is she now."

"She's dead. They found her body at the bottom of a ravine over looking Suda Bay."

"Murdered?" said Sam.

"They have no way of telling. The injuries are consistent with the fall but if she was pushed, jumped a just slipped there is no way of telling."

"I still don't understand how it took so long for us to find out that she was dead?" said Mandy.

"It's the way it was reported. It went through the Consular Office to the foreign office. We, on the other hand sent out a a person of interest notice to our European counterparts. She was already dead and they had already told us. The usual left and right hand not knowing what the other is doing."

"About right," said Sam.

"In any event that completes the set on Lost in Time members," said Merryweather.

"Not a group you want to find yourself in though is it. They are dying all over the place," said Siskin.

"We have no proof that Francis was murdered. Give us what the Greek police have found so far?" said Mandy.

Merryweather had printed the file off and flicked through. "As I said the forensics were inconclusive. She was last seen eating lunch in a local Taverna with a man. The description is fairly generic, thirties, average height and build and brownish hair."

"Well that fits, Reynolds, Ward and Hardy," said Sam.

"They drove off in her car after lunch and she wasn't seen again. The car was found a few days later in Heraklion, the Capital of the island."

"Well who drove it there?" said Mandy.

"There is no way of telling. She may have done so herself then and travelled to where she was found by some other means. Someone could have driven her and that need not have been the individual she had lunch with. The pathologist could not fix the time of death that precisely."

"Contents of her stomach?" said Mandy.

Realisation dawned on Merryweather's face. He checked the file. "The contents matched what she had for lunch, at the restaurant with her unknown companion. The food was hardly digested. You are right there wasn't time for her to have gone to Heraklion and then gone back using another means of transport to where the body was discovered."

"We have the scenario then. She arrives at the taverna in her car with her companion. They have lunch. They drive off. They go for a walk. She is probably pushed over the cliff by him. He takes her car and drives back to town and abandons the car. "Did they find her car keys on the her body?" said Mandy.

"No," said Merryweather.

"So there are two possibilities are there not?"

"He took the keys from her before he killed her or he had to climb down to where the body was and retrieve them," said Potts.

"So what did the search of the area reveal. If her killer had to climb down a rocky cliff then he might have left something, traces of skin, DNA or dropped something. Where did she usually keep her keys, in her bag? Did they test that?" said Mandy.

Merryweather flicked the pages of his printout. "None of the above, no finger tip search and no tests," he finally said.

"That's bloody fantastic," said Sam.

"Contact the Greek Police. We need them to go back and check the scene and we need them to check everything for DNA especially where she kept those car keys," said Mandy.

"I am not optimistic," said Merryweather. "You think we are struggling with budgetary constraints they are completely broke in Greece. They have cut pensions, pay and taken savings from depositors' bank accounts to stay afloat after the had to bailed out by the European Central bank. The County's essentially bust."

"Well can still do a lot this end. We have to assume that this is all linked to the murder of Millicent's baby. When did Francis die?" Mandy answered her own question. "Three days after the news that the baby's body had been found in Eastbourne. So she had time to see the reports on the television."

She paused as she reasoned the series of events in her mind, before continuing. "Right, here is what I think happened. She sees that the murder that she took some part in had been discovered. Now if she was merely a witness and not the perpetrator it would be to her advantage to come forward and get her version out there first. On the other hand she may have participated in the murder. Either way she makes contact with someone in the band and says she is going to go to the Police."

"We need to check all her phone calls and phone calls made by Reynolds, Ward and Hardy," said Sam.

"The perpetrator persuades her to hold off. His most persuasive line to achieve this would be that they needed to get their stories straight in order to minimise the consequences for them both. In any event he does manage to persuade her to hold off going straight to the police. "

"When we tried to arrange a meeting with Rod Hardy, their ex-manager, we were told he was away on business. So start with him. Track his travel movements," said Sam.

"We cannot just concentrate on him. We need to check the movements of Ward and Reynolds as well. Check all flight manifests and get copies of their bank accounts and credit card transactions. We have enough, as they are suspects in the murders of Bennet and Millicent's baby, to get authorisation. We have to assume that all the murders are linked and that the subsequent murder of Bennet and Francis are being carried out by the killer in an attempt to avoid detection."

"Anything else, boss?" said Sam.

Mandy looked at Sam. "That's the first time you have referred to me as boss. I am touched. Does that finally mean you think I might actually have some merit in the job?"

Sam reverted to his usual under the breath muttering as the team set to work.

Chapter 25

Mandy sat at her desk going through the files. She was struggling with the fact that if, as she suspected Millicent was still alive, she had not been found yet. They had found no bank account nor tax and NI records. In this day and age that seemed impossible. Everyone left a electronic footprint from mobile phones to online purchasing.

"What have we missed?"

"What did you say?" said Sam.

"Nothing really I was thinking out loud. I do not understand? Is it possible that Millicent Nook has died after she gave birth? Are we missing a body and another murder?"

"It is a possibility but how do we answer that? It is a seven year period and she could have died or been murdered anywhere and at anytime. If her body was not found there is no way to verify anything."

"She could have been found and another Police Force could have run a DNA search but as she was no longer officially missing they may not have obtained a match."

"No we have covered that. We have run our own search against any unidentified bodies. You are barking up the wrong tree."

"I just don't get it. She can't just disappear."

"People do go off the grid as they call it, use cash, work under the radar. It is the only way for some, like illegal immigrants. It is not that uncommon. You can even just walk into any hospital and get treatment, there are no checks to see who you are. They treat first and chase up after," said Sam.

Mandy sank back into her thoughts. Sam decided that he would get on with something else while she was doing thinking. He gathered up the files he had brought in and made for the door. He did not make it from her office.

"Illegal immigrants, that's it."

He camelback and sat down. "What's it?"

"She could be anywhere in the European Union, in any of the member states. Once you leave the UK you are in the Shengen Area. You can travel around the other twenty six member States without a passport."

"Surely you would need something to identify you to get a job, like an NI number or an identity card."

"I am sure you do but there are probably ways round it. Let's face it a lot of the new member states are not as particular in applying the law as the UK or don't have the best systems in place," she said.

"We have put out a EU wide search for her though."

"As you said she could be off the grid. The obvious area that a young girl could take to is the sex industry. From the picture we are getting of life in the flat she was earning money for herself and the other flat mates that way, keeping them in drugs. It would not be much of a leap of faith to imagine that she would turn it into a profession. She was essentially a young girl, with a drug habit and no means of income."

"Makes sense," said Sam. He rose and called to Potts and Siskin to come in.

"You have been tracking Lost in Time's touring schedule. Go back to the their first tour and tell me when and where they went after the date the baby was murdered. When was that June 2013?" said Mandy.

Ten minutes later Pott's came back with a stack of paper. They were the flyers advertising Lost in Time concerts abroad. He spread them across Mandy's desk and they began sifting through them. There were numerous different versions of poster and flyers advertising the same shows put out on various social media channels. After a bit of paper shuffling they had them sorted into chronological order.

"Right now we are getting somewhere," said Mandy. "Let's see where they went."

"The Netherlands," said Potts. "That is where started their first tour. There are photos and a sort of blog. I'll get my laptop."

Minutes later he returned and they gathered around the screen. "That's how they travelled, a minibus," said Sam.

"And Millicent could easily have travelled with them," said Mandy.

"Surely she would need a passport to get into the Netherlands?"

"Who knows there are many possibilities. They could have been waved through. She may have had one. She may have hidden on the bus. Let's face it most of the border checks are aimed at stopping people getting into the UK not the other way," she said.

"From Holland they went to Germany and then France and came back on the ferry from Calais."

"I think she left on that bus and did not come back. She could be anywhere in Europe and they may have no record of her being there especially if she is a sex worker."

"I was on holiday once and I had my passport stolen. I went to the Embassy and they can issue temporary travel documents to get you home. There was also some sort of system for issuing passports. My point is there are channels to get a passport without going through the UK Passport Office. She could have obtained a passport in another Country," said Potts.

"Or another Country's passport using some form of fake ID."

"We need to start with the Dutch Police, let's face it Amsterdam is the sex capital of Europe. Prostitution is legal and tolerated with light touch policing."

Potts left and passed Merryweather on the way in. "Forensics on the exhumation," he announced placing a sheet of paper on the table.

"As we thought, not Millicent," sad Sam.

Siskin appeared, "you should look at this." He handed another bit of paper to Sam.

"They have identified the body already. Her name is Charlotte Darmer. She was reported missing five days after the crash." said Sam. He handed the report to Mandy.

"Well it all begins to fit. She went out for the evening. Seems we have another troubled teen. She was in care and they had little control over her, usual MO, drinking, drugs and a history of absconding. No one took her disappearance that seriously because of her history of running off. She was from Bolton and had been placed in an unregulated care home. No support, more a less a bedsit, hundreds of miles form home," said Sam.

"My guess she went to the pub where Lost In Time where playing. She hooked up with Millicent somehow and ended up joyriding with her. Then the crash and the mess up in identity."

"It is sickening. Two girls, no more than children and this crap happens to them. You have to wonder about this Country sometimes, when we allow vulnerable kids to be treated like this," said Sam.

"Get onto the Dutch Police and see if we can't find Millicent," said Mandy.

Chapter 26

It had been a long day and for John Reynolds it was not finished yet. The last of the trucks had left the yard an hour before and yet another touring band's equipment was on its way. He finished double checking the paper work in his office before locking up.

He drove his Mercedes to the barrier and waved goodnight to the security guard before driving onto the M25 and heading towards Eastbourne. His mind was racing with doubt. The phone call he had revived earlier in the day had been in equal measure intriguing and frightening.

Since the visit by the Police he had been expecting something but not this. He knew that there was always the threat of the body of Millicent's baby being discovered and that the police would come knocking. He had forced it to the back of his mind and as time passed he felt danger fade. Now one phone call had changed all that.

After the events of that fateful night they had never mentioned it again. It was though it had never happened. It was as if they never spoke of it then it would go away. It had been so for years but of course these things never really go away. He knew that and tonight he had to deal with it.

Before setting off he had entered the coordinates in the sat nav. He did not really need to. He knew the area well, Norman's Bay. It was a little to the east of Eastbourne itself. There was a camp site. It was not in use this time of year. It was a good spot for a meeting, quiet and away from the ever present CCTV coverage that grew daily in the UK.

He turned off the M25 and headed for Tonbridge Wells. He checked the clock on the dash. He was ahead of time and would arrive early he thought but the traffic through the town put paid to that. As he emerged the other side of Tonbridge Wells he found himself running late. He increased his speed in an attempt to make up the time.

He felt a knot of fear as he turned off the by pass and headed down the small lanes that led to the bay. He did not know what he would say. What defence he or anyone could offer. He was not even sure in his own mind what had happened. The drugs made it all so confusing. It had been a period of madness in his life, not just in his life but all their lives.

He switched his headlights to full beam and slowed the car. There was no street lighting and no moon tonight. The dark shadows and silence made the journey unreal. It felt as though the car was floating in a sea of darkness. He strained forward in his seat looking for the agreed meeting spot. It way no more than a pull in before the clubhouse and entrance to the campsite.

He started. He saw the figure in the beam of the headlights barely discernable in the shadows. He pulled the car to a halt. He sat and waited gaining his composure before opening the door. The figure remained in the shadows, unmoving placing the onus on him to make the first movement. He closed the door to the car and taking a deep breath made his way across the car park. It was hard to see in the darkness. When the interior light faded and went out it took a while for his eyes to adjust and for a brief moment he felt panic in the dark of night.

They stood face to face. The silence only broken by the sound of distant waves lapping on the beach behind them. The silence continued and it was clear that he would need to speak first. "How did you find me?" he said.

"That was easy. You know why we are here?"

"I am not sure what I can say. I am not sure what you want to hear," he said.

"You do know really. You just do not want to admit it."

"I am not sure. It was a long time ago. It was confused. I find it hard to see the reality from the hallucinations."

"Oh, you know," came the reply.

He did know but he had hid it for so long it did not seem tangible. It was more of a dream or more accurately a nightmare. He had hoped and prayed that this day would never come. He had hoped that it was over. Of course it would never be over.

"It is time to come to terms and pay the price," the voice said from the darkness.

"We all need to take responsibility for that night," he said.

"Tonight is when you take yours."

"I am not going to the police. They can't prove anything, no one can." He felt the defiance in his voice. He had guilt but at heart he was like most animals. He was selfish and put his own preservation first. He had a life now, a family and a business. He had no desire to face the consequences of what had happened when he was young and naïve.

"I am not suggesting you should. The time for that is long gone. It won't change anything. It wouldn't undo anything. It would not bring back the dead. No that is not the reason we are here."

"What do you want then? Why are we here? I don't understand what I can give you that would mean anything."

"Only this," said the voice in the darkness.

At first he did not understand what had happened. The figure had moved close to him as they spoke. He could feel the breath on the night air as they spoke. He had not seen the knife, the sudden movement as it was thrust into him. He felt what he thought to be a light push to his chest. Then he finally understood.

He clutched at the wound. Blood ran through his fingers. He started to choke as the blood filled his lungs. The second stab wound was to his back as he doubled forward gasping for air. The third stab wound was to the back of his neck. He fell to the gravel, his face and body contorted in pain as the figure walked away.

The last thing he heard was the car driving away as his life drained from him, drop by drop, beat by beat.

Chapter 27

The rain was pelting down and the wind almost at gale force as Mandy and Sam pulled up at the crime scene. There was flooding in across the UK, particularly in coastal regions. Rivers had burst their banks. further North, towns and villages were already underwater. "There goes my new hairstyle," said Mandy opening the car door and making her way towards the taped off area.

Sam said nothing apart from his usual grunt, a cross between a mumble and a moan as he got out and was confronted by the wind. The lane was already partially flooded and the waves in the distance could be seen pounding the pebble beach. Everywhere was bathed in a dim grey light.

The Constable stationed at the entrance to the parking area was dripping wet and shivered slightly as they approached. "Nice weather for it," said Sam as they passed him.

"I'm taking the kids for a picnic and a swim later," came the reply.

Making their way across the gravel, lay-bye, she said. "Why do the English say the opposite to what they mean? I had a German friend at University and she spent the entire three years in a state of confusion. Once she was so happy that she had done well in an essay she expected to do badly in. The tutor returning the work had said ironically, that went well didn't it? She spent the rest of the day thinking she had passed and was surprised to see she had not."

"Why would he say it had gone well, when it had gone so badly? She asked me later."

"You have to admit if you live here for any length of time you come to expect things to be rubbish. Let's face it. there is a great deal of room for disappointment if you're English. Penalty shoot outs, we lose. Rugby World Cup finals, we lose. Referendum on leaving the European Union a draw. Catching a train from Eastbourne to London, there is more chance of the second coming than that."

"You have a point." Mandy approached the forensic team leader. "Now tell me. You have DNA, made a match, identified the killer and can give us his address."

The young woman dressed in a soggy white coverall looked confused. "It's the English way," said Sam. "She doesn't mean it. She expects you to have found nothing, that you can't determine the method, time of death nor how the deceased got here."

"He drove. That's his car," she pointed to the Mercedes ten yards away.

"And?" said Mandy.

"That's about it. He was stabbed last night, the rain has probably washed away any other evidence. We have found nothing."

"Well done. That went well then," said Mandy to a confused and very wet crime of scene investigator.

"You might just be overdoing the English understatement," said Sam.

They approached the body of John Reynolds. A small tent like canopy had been erected over the body. The rain had done its work. The blood had been washed away and the body lay in a small puddle. There was little to be gleaned at the scene. They would have to wait and see if the laboratory report turned up any further evidence.

They made their way back to the car leaving forensics to finish up and move the body to the autopsy room."The body count seems to be on the up," said Sam.

"It is running away with itself, first the baby, then a burnt girl in a car, then Adrian Bennet, possibly Francis Donally and now John

Reynolds," she said.

"It does sort of narrow the field as to suspects though," said Sam engaging drive in the car and heading along the coast to the Police Station.

"Looking at it that way, we only had the Lost in Time band members and their Manager Rod Hardy," she said.

"So it has to be Peter Ward or Rod Hardy, simples," said Sam.

"Or Millicent, don't forget she may be somewhere around, looking for revenge on the people who murdered her baby."

"Three suspects, it is not usually that easy."

"Well it is most of the time. Let's face it most murders are committed by family members or close associates of the victim, ex-partners, wives or husbands. Apart from gang related violence or arguments in the car, in a pub or club your average murder stays with in a relatively narrow band width. You don't get many random killings."

"Yeah you're right. The problem is getting the evidence and proving it beyond a reasonable doubt."

"We are high on theories and a possible motive here but sadly lacking in any sort of evidence so far," said Mandy.

"The case against Millicent is a bit thin in any event. Whatever happened to her baby at the flat, happened a long while ago. Why would she suddenly decide now is the time to take revenge on her former flat mates?" said Sam.

"Perhaps it was the discovery of the body. It may have been some sort of trigger. You know she had suppressed it all these years but seeing the news coverage it came flooding back. Filled with hate she goes on a killing spree."

"We are not even sure she is still alive. Even if she is there has been no sightings of a knife waving woman wondering about. We can't place anyone at either Bennet's or Reynold's murder. We can't be one hundred percent how and if Francis Donally was murdered in Crete."

"It's going well then," laughed Mandy.

"Enough of the English irony," Sam laughed.

"Okay," said Mandy. Let's go and have a word with Mr Peter Ward and Mr Rod Hardy.

Chapter 28

Mandy and Sam stood looking at the CCTV in Eastbourne Police Station. They were watching Rod Hardy sitting patiently behind the desk, in the interview room. "That was handy," said Mandy.

"Certainly was, saved us another encounter with Southern Railways and a trip to London," said Sam.

"So how is he here?"

"I rang his office and they said he was away but gave me his mobile. I rang it obviously, to arrange an interview. It turns out he was here in Eastbourne. He said he would come to the station. As they say 'Bob's your uncle' and here he is."

Mandy and Sam took up their positions in the seats on the opposite side of the desk to Hardy. "Thank you for coming in Mr Hardy, as you know I am DCI Pile and this is DS Shaw. We are hopeful that you may be able to help us shed some light on a number of matters we are currently investigating."

"I am always happy to be assistance to the Police. How may I help?" He looked far from happy and Mandy was fairly sure that he was unlikely to be of any assistance at all, if he could avoid it.

"Last night John Reynold was murdered in a lay-bye near Norman's Bay. As you were a known associate of his, we should like to know your movements around the time of his murder."

He looked less than surprised at the news of Reynolds murder. "I saw it on social media this morning. That why I hung around here. I guessed you might like to talk to me."

"That was considerate of you. Let's start with how you come to be in Eastbourne, shall we?"

"I had a meeting at Glyndebourne."

"Where they hold the opera malarkey?" said Sam.

"The Glyndebourne Festival or opera malarkey as you put it, yes that's the place. They have started expanding from the classical into the popular. They have put on other more contemporary artists in the past. Anyway, I am in discussion with them to stage a concert with some of the artists I manage."

"I see. So you came down from London when?" said Mandy.

"Yesterday morning, I had the meeting and had lunch with my hosts."

"And then, what were you movements?"

"I drove back to Eastbourne and checked into the Best Western on the seafront at about six o'clock."

"What car do you drive?" said Sam.

"A Jaguar F Pace," he replied. Sam made a note of the car license plate number, which he would later run against the automatic number plate recognition system to track its movements on the various cameras linked to the system.

"Go on, what next?" urged Mandy.

"I went to my room first and then later met up with and old friend at around seven thirty. We had diner together and I returned around ten thirty and went to bed."

"This old friend does he have a name?"

"Peter Ward," he said.

Mandy and Sam looked at each other, both their suspects in the murder of John Reynolds were together at around the time of his death. "Was there a specific reason why you and Mr Ward met?" said Mandy.

"No not really we were just catching up. As you know, he was in Lost in Time, who I had some success with."

"Do you met regularly?"

"No not often, just when the opportunity affords itself. We are both quite busy people."

"In fact you haven't met since the band broke up. It was quite an acrimonious split was it not? I mean there were law suits and allegations of you mismanaging the finances?"

"These things happen in business. People always think they should have had more money. It is the nature of the beast."

"But despite the allegations and legal battles you remained friends?" said Sam sounding more than cynical in his comment.

"Well time is a great healer and it was a while ago," Hardy shrugged his shoulders and put out his arms, turning his palms upwards. It was a gesture of, 'you know how it is'.

"I would suggest that your meeting had to do with recent events concerning the body of baby discovered in your flat in Eastbourne and where Mr Ward lived at the time."

"I have already told you. I was never resident there. I knew nothing about a baby."

"So you have. You also have no recollection of what happened to the mother of the baby, Millicent Nook, yet she lived there and we have found photos, on line of her with the band on tours you clearly arranged."

Nicholas E Watkins

Hardy sat silently for a moment before replying. "Do I need a lawyer am I being accused if anything?"

"I don't know if you need a lawyer, you can have one present by all means. If you are guilty of something it would be a good idea. What are you guilty of Mr Hardy the murder of Adrian Bennet, Francis Donally, John Reynolds or Millicent's baby?" said Sam

Some of the arrogance and confidence left his demeanour. "I have done nothing wrong."

"In that case we can continue," said Mandy. "So you had dinner with Mr Ward and returned to the hotel. Did you go out again?"

"No I stayed in my room until this morning." The hotel and restaurant would be followed up and the alibi checked after the interview.

"Have you visited Crete recently?"

"No, why are you asking?" he genuinely seemed puzzled.

"The body of Francis Donally as been discovered in Crete by the Greek Police. When we had our first interviewed you we were told that you had been out of the Country and had returned just prior to us speaking with you, Where had you been?"

"I had no idea she was dead. I had nothing to do with it." He appeared to be visibly shaken by the news. I was in Paris and then travelled to Berlin, back to Paris then home. I was meeting with promoters to organise a tour for acts I manage. My personal assistant can give you the full itinerary."

"And you are adamant that you never went to Crete?"

"I am sure. You can check," he said.

"Rest assured we will," said Sam, "I think though that you are pretty savvy and know that once in the Shengen Area it will be difficult as there are no passport checks. It you do it the right way, use cash, avoid airlines and car hire companies, it is pretty easy to travel about without leaving a paper trail."

"Let's just explore Adrian Bennet's murder. We are still checking you alibi at this stage, Do you still deny any involvement is his murder?"

"Of course I do." He said.

"The things that bothers us is that the link between the deaths of Francis, Bennet and Reynolds is the circumstances surrounding the murder of the baby. Now here's the thing Mr Hardy. Earlier in this interview I refereed to the murder of Millicent Nook's baby. You showed no reaction. When we met at your offices you denied knowing her or of her. I think we all know that you knew her, didn't you?"

"Would you like that lawyer now?" said Sam.

Rod Hardy looked ruffled for the first time in the interview. It was clear that he realised that he had been caught in a lie. The dilemma that faced him was that he could not be sure what the police did or did not know. What they had as fact, what they had pieced together,what was conjecture and superstition. He ignored Sam's question as to having a lawyer present. He finally spoke.

"It came up in conversation with Peter last night. He reminded me about her. I vaguely recall now seeing her at the flat," he said.

"Do you vaguely recall going to a gig in the Midlands with her and Lost in Time?"

"There were many gigs, all over the Country and lots of girls hanging around the band at the time."

"Yes this was a bit special wasn't it. Perhaps you could try a little harder to remember after all it was the night that Millicent Nook died."

"I honestly don't know what happened that night. I went to the venue. I saw the band set up. I dealt with the finances and left them to it. They were due to drive back the next day after the show. I think I checked into a cheap hotel somewhere."

"Right, you can see how we find that a little difficult to believe. Don't you? You again showed no surprise at my statement that Millicent died that night. You knew what happened."

"No not really, I knew something had happened after, when I went to the flat, I think a few days after. They were all sort of laughing. I asked what the joke was. They showed me a newspaper which carried the story of this girl's death. I didn't really make the connection at the time. The flat was an open house, girls were coming and going all the time. To be honest I didn't want to know. I just ignored it. It was only speaking with John ward that I made the connection between the baby, Millicent and the dead girl in the car fire."

Mandy and Sam sat in the interview room. Hardy had left. "What do you make of that?" said Sam.

"He's lying of course. He knew about Millicent being there and the mistaken identity of the dead girl. The question is can we put him at the scene, when the baby was murdered? Can we place him in Crete, where Francis Donally was murdered? Can we place him at Bennet's or Reynold's murder? No we can't."

"We can have a bloody good try though. We will go over it all again, flights, car movements, CCTV, credit card and bank transactions. If its there to be found we will find it," said Sam.

"I know that but there is something missing. I told you there is something in the back of my mind I just can't pin point it. Something I saw. It will come to me eventually."

Chapter 29

"Right Mr Ward," said Mandy. "I assume you know whey we have asked you to come to the Station?"

Peter Ward was occupying the same chair in the interview room that had been vacated two hours earlier by Rod Hardy. He looked less self assured than his predecessor but still in command of his emotions. "I heard of the death of John Reynolds," he replied.

"Can you tell us what you did yesterday evening," said Sam?

"I know you have spoken to Rod. You know exactly what I did."

"So he phoned you after his interview? Was that an attempt to get your stories straight?" said Sam.

"No, of course not, it was the normal thing to do. If you had been interviewed by the police wouldn't you let your friend know what was going on?"

"Perhaps," said Mandy. "Anyway, we need you to tell us exactly what you did. If you don't mind?" They sat and listened as he confirmed Hardy's account of events. They met at seven thirty, had diner and went their separate ways.

"What time did you return home?" The timings he gave were a match to those given by Ward and his subsequent movements left no time for him to get to Norman's Bay, kill Reynolds and be home at the time his wife would corroborate his arrival there.

"Now what we should like to know is the real reason you met with Mr Hardy. After all it is not as though you are close friends. You have hardly spoke since Lost in Time split and when you have it was more an acrimonious argument over money, wasn't it?" said Mandy.

"He was around and it was time to bury the hatchet."

"Or as we suspect to discuss the finding of a baby's body in the flat you and the rest of the band occupied?" said Sam.

He look flustered. He thought for a while before replying. "Yes we both saw it on the news and we did discuss it. Neither of us knew anything about a baby."

"Did you during the course of these discussions over diner come to a conclusion as to who murdered the baby? Was it you?" said Mandy.

"No I did not. I don't recall any baby and certainly not a murder." He was beginning to become agitated and a small drop of sweat appeared on his top lip.

"And Millicent Nook?" said Mandy.

"The young woman who hung out with the band?"

"Girl, Mr Ward, a girl of fourteen who you and your fellow band members took advantage of. She lived at the flat, became pregnant, had a baby which was murdered and boarded up in a hole in the wall. I ask you again tell us about Millicent."

"Alright I do remember her vaguely. You have to understand it was all so chaotic back then. There was the drink and drugs, people came and went all the time. It was out of control. It was a haze, a blur. Now it does not even seem part of this life."

"So Lost in Time, so to speak," said Mandy. He sat silently and waited for the next question. "You can see that we find it hard to understand how a young girl, a runaway, lives with you all, follows you to you gigs, even travels with you but seems to have been erased from your collective memory, don't you?"

"I wasn't that close to her. She was more Francis's and Johns's friend."

"But you had sex with her." said Sam.

"She was under aged, so no of course not."

"Of course not, that is very convenient now that you are heading up the Child Section of Social Services. I understand that you are in line for the top job for the whole of East Sussex aren't you?" Sam continued.

Ward's face turned white and his eyes darted from side to side as though looking for the exit. "I deny any part of it. I had nothing to do with it."

"Tell me about the car crash. Were you driving?" said Mandy.

Ward was looking more and more like a trapped rat searching for a way out. He was visibly shaken and his voice trembled slightly as he responded. "I don't know what you are talking about."

Mandy let the tension build, letting his answer hang in the air. She pushed the photo downloaded from the net showing Millicent with the band towards him. "Do you recognise yourself and Millicent in this photo? Are you trying to deny that Millicent was with you when the band performed at the Lady Godiva Pub in Coventry?"

"She may have been," he said.

"Really, is that your reply? She may have been. Come now you can do better than that," said Sam.

"It was a long time ago," he realised his answer sounded unconvincing.

"I put it to you that you, the band and Millicent all drove to Coventry for the performance. After you had played your gig you all went to a local takeaway. One of you decided that you would round off the evening by stealing a car, going for a joyride. Millicent was in that car along with a local girl. Who else was in that car? Who was the driver? Was it you?"

It was clear that Ward was struggling under the questioning. He was visibly sweating now and his hands were beginning to tremble. "I did not steal a car or crash a car."

Mandy let the silence hang to allow time for the words he had just uttered have time for him to absorb. "So while you cannot recall anything else you can remember a car that you deny stealing that crashed. How do you explain that?"

He realised that he had partly incriminated himself. "I must have read about or seen it on the TV."

"Then you would have read that a girl was killed in that crash. That girl was assumed to be Millicent."

"I don't remember that," his replies were becoming increasingly implausible and the look of desperation was self evident in his behaviour.

Mandy paused increasing the tension in the room before speaking emphasising each contradiction. "You can understand how I am struggling to believe your statement. There is no denying that a car was stolen. It crashed and a girl was killed. We know that girl was not Millicent. We believe the girl that was killed and burnt in the car crash was Charlotte Darmer. What we don't know is who the driver was."

"I did not steal any car. I know nothing about it."

"If we accept the first part of that statement it means the second part must be a lie," said Mandy.

Ward looked puzzled. "I don't understand," he finally said.

"Then I shall lay it out for you. As the Millicent returned to Eastbourne, where she subsequently gave birth, she and the driver of the car had to have got back somehow. We have ruled out all possible options as to how they left the crash site, bus, taxi, ambulance or a passing motorist. So how did the driver of the stolen car and Millicent arrive back here?"

Ward remained impassive. Mandy continued. "There was a phone call that pinged a tower. The driver or Millicent phoned someone in the band. They went in the band's touring van and picked them up. So you see that even if you weren't the driver and stole the car, you must have known what had transpired because you were in the vehicle that drove to the crash site. So let's try again. Did you steal the car and crash killing Charlotte Darmer if not who was it?"

He had no choice but to deny it again which he did. To keep him off balance Mandy switched tact. "Do you keep in touch with Francis Donally"

He shook his head. "I don't know where she is even."

"She's was in Crete," said Sam. "So if we examine your phone and internet records we won't see any communications with here?"

"I did not know she was in Crete and you are welcome to check my phone."

"You left the Country recently?" said Mandy.

"I went to Brussels for an EU sponsored summit on child welfare. So?"

"Your went via Paris. Did you know that Mr Hardy was there at the same time?"

"No I didn't. I didn't meet him, if that is what you are suggesting?"

"No that is not the suggestion. Did you by chance make a detour to the Island of Crete?" said Mandy.

"No of course not, why?"

"Because somebody did. Francis Donally's body has been found and she died around the time you and Mr Hardy were out of the UK."

"I am not answering any more questions without a lawyer," said Peter Ward.

"In that case you are free to leave, but don't plan any trips without letting us know first," said Sam.

Chapter 30

The atmosphere in the room was tense. Superintendent Taylor was sitting in Mandy's chair when she and Sam entered her office. She took the seat opposite. Sam remained standing. "Well," he said and waited for a response.

"Well," said Mandy."We are developing lines of enquiry."

"We really need some progress. We seem to have started with the body of a baby, killed many years ago but now we seem to be having bodies popping up left, right and centre. We are supposed to be solving murders not creating them." Sam almost smiled but realised in time that Taylor, although a man of many qualities a sense of humour was not among them.

"They are obviously linked," said Mandy.

"Enlighten me."

"We have the following suspects in the murder. Firstly Millicent, the mother, initially we could not see how as she seemed to have predeceased the infant's death. Upon investigation we found that the DNA identification of her body in a car fire was flawed and another girl called Christine Darmer was in fact the victim."

"That I admit was excellent detective work," said Taylor. "How did it lead to the other deaths and murders?"

"The conclusion we are working on is that the subsequent deaths are an attempt to cover up the killing of the baby. It is apparent that the suspects are limited, the members of the band, Lost in Time and their manager Rod Hardy. The band comprised, Francis Donally, John Reynolds, Adrian Bennet and Peter Ward. The most likely suspect of course, who had to have been present was the baby's mother Millicent Nook."

"Well your list of suspects seems to be getting shorter daily," Sam almost took this as a joke but stopped himself laughing in the nick of time.

"We cannot be sure of the cause of death but Francis Donally appears to have been the first. She died within days of Millicent's baby being discovered. My guess is that she was the weakest link and contacted someone and said that she was going to the police. I am guessing that she saw the news report and had a crisis of conscience.

"And someone went to Crete and pushed her over a cliff," said Taylor," That seems a reasonable assumption."

"So here's our problem, apart from Adrian Bennet who was wheelchair bound, we cannot rule out any of the rest as suspects in her death. John Reynolds was a haulier who transports the kit for bands all over the World. Rod Hardy globe trots, organising gigs for the bands he manages. Peter Ward was on the Continent at a Conference. They were all out of the Country at the time of her death."

"We are trying to track their movements with the help of our colleagues in Europe but as you can guess it is not easy and even less likely to be definitive. Anyone of them could have visited Crete undetected if they took simple precautions like using cash and not flying," said Sam.

"Next to be taken out of the equation was Adrian Bennet," said Mandy.

"Was there any indication that he was going to come forward and identify the baby's killer?" said Taylor.

"That's the odd thing. When we questioned him, I did not get the impression that he was going to give us any help. In fact he played up his inability to speak clearly and denied any knowledge of the death."

"But he was murdered, any clues" said Taylor?

"We have to assume that his conscious got the better of him, had a change of heart and was going to talk to us. He was silenced at that point. There is no record of him contacting the other suspects before his death so it seems he was killed as a precaution."

"That seems a bit drastic. I mean, if there was no evidence that he was going to talk to us and incriminate someone."

"The only clue to his murder in that a neighbour saw a Volkswagen car that he thought belonged to the nurse that called on him daily. We know that it was not her car as she had left much earlier. We are looking for that car still."

"Peter Ward does have a Volkswagen," said Sam.

"But he also has a alibi. He says he was at home with his wife," said Mandy.

"Then John Reynolds turns up dead in Eastbourne," said Taylor.

"The suspects have to be Peter Ward, the last remaining member of Lost in Time and their manager Rod Hardy. Unfortunately they alibi each other. We have no forensic, the rain cleaned the scene pretty much and no CCTV," said Mandy.

"We are checking CCTV wider and wider spreading out from Eastbourne. If the murderer of Adrian Benett and John Reynolds are the same person, we are looking for a Volkswagen being driven in and around Eastbourne at the time of his death," said Sam.

"That leaves one person still unaccounted for, Millicent," said Mandy. "She runs away from home and somehow ends up squatting with the band. Now none of them want to admit to anything about her. The life style in that flat was chaotic. It was a mixture of a drug house and a knocking shop. They seemed to be living off of the money earned by a combination of Francis and Millicent turning tricks and dealing drugs. Millicent was under aged and I am guessing they all took their fair share of sexual enjoyment with her. None of them will admit that of course and all claimed a collective loss of memory when it comes to her actually being at the flat at all."

"We think one of them got her pregnant," said Sam.

"And one of them killed the baby, when it was born and hid her in a hole in the wall when it was born?" said Taylor.

"Or Millicent killed the baby herself and they covered it up," said Mandy. "In any event they all have a strong motive for murder to stop the truth coming out," said Taylor.

"It is fortuitous you came today," said Mandy.

Taylor was less than convinced by her statement. In truth he had the impression that she and Sam were less than happy at finding him in her office.

"I have just been handed this." She passed the email to Taylor. "The Dutch Police have an address for Millicent Nook. She is living in Amsterdam as far as we know."

"Why did it take so long to find her?" said Taylor. "She is using a UK passport surely?"

"Yes she just applied for one by the looks of it," said Mandy looking at the passport application form Potts had just obtained and passed to her before she had entered her office. "It was issued after she was declared dead and about three months after she had the baby."

"How's that possible," said Taylor.

"It's very possible apparently. She put in her application in the normal way and they issued her a passport. There was no reason not too. What is there to connect a dead girl in the car crash and a school girl by the same name applying for her first passport, nothing."

"So our prime suspect is living in Amsterdam," said Taylor. "You had better go and speak to her.

"Thank you that what I was going to ask you, authorise the cost of the the trip."

Chapter 31

"What is that you are eating now?" said Mandy.

"I am not sure. It like a croquette sort of thing," said Sam as he bit into a ball of something coated in breadcrumbs. It split and liquid dribbled down his chin. "it is really nice though. I think it is called a bitter ball or something like that."

"Right," said Mandy, "Is there any chance that we called meet the Dutch Police without you being covered in gravy and crumbs?" They had been at Skipol airport for twenty minutes awaiting Inspector Herbert of the Dutch Police. It had been agreed that they would accompany him to the address where Millicent had been traced to in Amsterdam.

They had insufficient grounds to issue an international arrest warrant and after a long telephone discussion it had been decided that the only realistic approach would be for Sam and Mandy to go with the local Police and interview Millicent about the death of her baby.

"I missed breakfast," said Sam. "Do you think I have time to nip back in and get another one of whatever that was?"

Before she could reply a police car pulled up. "Saved by the Police yet again," she said. The door opened and Inspector Herbert stepped from the passenger side to greet them. Hands were shaken all round and with Sam and Mandy in the rear, the car drove off to Amsterdam.

Sam was more interested in his belated breakfast than the case. "What was that I just ate, bitter balls?"

"Bitterballen," said Herbert. "Its a sort of stew. It's frozen, rolled in breadcrumbs and deep fried. You need to be careful when you eat it. It's very hot in the middle and can squirt everywhere." He looked at Sam's tie and deduced that he had already worked the last part out for himself.

"I like to try the local food when I travel," said Sam. Mandy was unsure as to how she could switch the conversation to the case and Millicent. It seemed as if the Dutch and English police were bonding over great snacks they had eaten. The conversation had now switched to slagroom

"Slagroom is wonderful. We just eat it piled thick between waffles. I will get you some when we have a chance. It is beaten cream." said Herbert.

"whipped," said Sam.

"Slaag means to hit or beat in Dutch."

Mandy contained her impatience a while longer while the qualities of the Dutch equivalent of Chantilly cream was fully discussed between them. Finally she felt she could turn the conversation for the reason for their trip to the Netherlands. "What do you have on Millicent Nook?"

Reluctantly Inspector Herbert turned his attention to her. The conversation with Sam was at that stage on pindasaus, the Dutch equivalent of satay sauce, which apparently was a must with chips, if mayonnaise was not selected as the first choice accompaniment.

"Not much really, she has done nothing to bring herself to our attention. She works as a prostitute along with hundreds of other girls from around the World in Amsterdam. She is only on record because she was attacked and badly beaten some years back. That's how she flagged up when your team sent out their requests for information."

"Do you know when she arrived in the Netherlands?"

"No, she is an EU citizen, there is no need."

"Are you sure she is at this address? She hasn't moved.?"

"Pretty sure, she goes for regular check ups for sexually transmitted diseases like most of the working girls. We got her address from the medical record," replied Herbert.

The driver manoeuvred the police car between a flock of cyclists and over a narrow bridge, turning parallel to the canal. "This is the main red light district. Her apartment is not far."

Moments later the car came to a halt. They all stepped from the car along with the driver, who was the only one in uniform. Even though it was not even lunch time there were girls on display in the windows and pimps encouraging tourists to experience the attractions on offer.

"It's busy here. Is it always like this?" said Mandy.

"Oh yes, sex is very popular as a pastime in Holland," said Herbert as the made their way to the building where Millicent lived. "These used to be merchants houses in the old days. Now of course they have been broken up into apartments. You see how narrow they are. Those protruding timber structures under the eves were used to haul goods and furniture up from the street and canals into the upper floors. You attach a block and tackle and you are ready to go."

The front door was open. They were immediacy confronted by a

149

narrow staircase that wound its way up through the building. The need to bring goods in through the windows became obvious. There was no way you could get a sofa up the narrow stairway. There was enough room for the four police officers to ascend however.

"This is her flat." said Herbert. The uniformed officer banged on the door.

There was no response. "Polizei," he shouted knocking harder.

"It's a long way to come to find no one at home," said Sam.

"Have you noticed that smell?" said Mandy.

"Are you trying to suggest you can smell gas so we need to break in for public safety," said Herbert. "I am not sure about that.."

"No, can't you smell it?"

"Sam and the two Dutch policemen shook their heads. "I can't smell anything," said Sam.

"Well I can and its isn't gas. I know that smell. Once you have smelt it you never forget it." She turned to Sam." Knock the door in."

Inspector Herbert looked slightly alarmed as Sam stepped forward. He looked at the door. "I could just open it," he said. He removed a credit card from his wallet and within moments had slipped the latch. "You do learn a few thins about breaking and entering after a few years in this job."

He gave the door a gentle push and it swung back. They stepped back. The stench was overwhelming. The was no mistaking the distinct odour of decomposition. They instantly knew that the flat contained a dead body. A dead body that had been dead sometime.

Herbert entered first and had a gun in his hand. The uniformed policeman followed also with weapon drawn. There was a small hallway that had the bathroom to one side and a single door into the living area, with bed, chair, a small table and a kitchenette.

Sat in the chair was the body of Millicent Nook. The smell was atrocious. There was a swarm of flies buzzing everywhere and bodily fluids were oozing onto the floor and carpet. Herbert draw plastic gloves from his pocket and put then on. The rest apart from Sam put their hands over their noses.

Inspector Herbert approached the body. He noticed the blackened spoon, scorched, stained cotton wool and in foil lying next to her. Her arm hand a belt twisted around it and the needle still protruded from a vein. "Looks like she overdosed on heroine," he said.

Chapter 32

Mandy and Sam left the short stay parking at Gatwick and drove south towards Brighton and Eastbourne. It was already dark when they joined the M23 motorway. They had cut short their intended investigations in Amsterdam. Millicent's death was a matter for the Dutch police. Their initial assessment was that there was no foul play. She had died of an heroine overdose. There was no telling if it was accidental or deliberate. Mandy suspected the latter. The timing was too much of a coincidence. She had died within a day of her baby being found walled up in the flat in Eastbourne.

Sam was driving. "So you think she saw the news of her baby and then killed herself?"

"The timing would seem to bear that out."

"Why had she not done so years before? She must have known? After all even if she didn't actually commit the murder she had to have taken part in the cover up? So it was hardly a surprise was it?"

"We may never know the answers. Something went on in that flat but unless we can get Ward or Hardy to tell us we have no way or finding out. We may never solve what actually happened."

"So we concentrate on the murders of Donally, Bennet and Reynolds," said Sam.

"One thing that struck me as odd was that Reynolds, Ward and Hardy were out of the Country at the time of Francis Donally's death,"

said Mandy.

"There all had reasons. Reynolds moving equipment around for touring pop bands, Ward at a conference on Social Care or something and Hardy promoting his acts."

"I am not so much questioning their activities but their motivation, why then? We need to check if those trips were last minute? Were they a smokescreen to cover Donally's murder?" said Mandy.

"So you are thinking that Donally, seeing the baby's death on the News, riddled with guilt decides she is going to the police. She emails of telephones one of her former band members and tells them what she is about to do. They get together and come up with a plan to rid themselves of the threat," said Sam.

"They are not stupid. They realise that if they jumped on a plane to Crete they would be rumbled as soon as we started checking the flight manifests. So they all head off to the Continent within days of each other. Once they are in the Schengen area they know they can travel undetected not having to produce passports as they cross borders."

"We need to tract their every movement after they left the UK," said Sam.

"We can't, can we? That's the point. We can't ask half the police forces in Europe to spend hours and thousands of Euros in resources on the off chance that one of our suspects may or may not have crossed their borders and may or may not have murdered someone in Crete."

"So its down to the Greek police to investigate. They are more cash strapped than we are."

"I agree. There is very little chance that they will investigate the matter further. My impression was that with no real evidence to the contrary they are happy to let her death remain as an accident."

"So we can forget about her and Millicent. It is not in our hands," said Sam.

"We can still go after the killer of Bennett and Reynolds though," said Mandy.

"Well, however you look at it we only have two realistic suspects, Ward and Hardy."

"And nothing linking them to the murders, no witnesses, no CCTV and no forensics."

"My thinking is that they are in it together. Both have a lot to lose," said Sam. "Say Francis, as you say, phones one of the ex Lost in Time, band members or their manger Rod Hardy. Ward and Hardy come up with the plan to silence her. Bennet perhaps had nothing to do with the murder and disposal of the baby and won't go along with it. Having dealt with Francis Donally they would have no choice but to silence him as well," said Sam.

"And Reynolds, he had to be part of the plan to kill Donally. He left the country as well and might actually have pushed her over the cliff. So why did they kill him?" said Mandy.

Sam sat silently driving. They were coming up to the Langley roundabout and were about five minutes from Emma Nooks home. "Perhaps he got cold feet and had a change of heart?"

"None of it really holds together," said Mandy. "There was a clear motive to rid themselves of Donally if she was going to go to the police. There is no reason to assume that Ward, Reynolds, Bennet or Hardy suddenly had an attack of conscience. No my reading was that they did not give one jot about what happened to Millicent or her baby. All of them have been evasive and obstructive from the get go. The only time they have given us a scrape of information or help is when we have forced it out of them, I cannot see either one of them even contemplating coming clean about the events in that flat. They are fully signed up members of the me first club."

"Here we are,"said Sam as they turned into the road where Emma Nook, Millicent's mum, lived. "Have you ever seen so many clapped out bangers in one place, outside a scrapyard. Some of these cars haven't been made since Moses parted the Red Sea. Look at the state of that Renault," he grumbled as he struggled to find a place to park. "That Vauxhall and that Volkswagen should be in a scrape yard and look at that Toyota it has so much rust, even the body filler has rust. I have a good mind to call traffic and get them to do a vehicle check. When they finish there will be plenty of space to park. Most of these cars would be in the crusher."

"You do enjoy a good moan," said Mandy as the finally found a spot and stepped from the car.

"Do you want to do this now?" said Sam as they made their way to Emma Nook's house.

"I think so. I don't want to leave it to the family liaison officers. We gave her hope. We told her we thought Millicent may still be alive and now we have to tell that we have found her."

"And that she is dead, probably though a heroine overdose?" said Sam.

"There is no easy way to deal with the truth but delaying won't make it any better."

The Station had phoned ahead to ensure Emma was at home for Mandy's arrival. She was on days at the Hospital, where she worked as a nurse. The door opened as they approached it. Emma showed them in and they sat. There was a moment's awkward silence while Mandy searched for the right words.

"I am not sure how to tell you this. We found Millicent. She had been living in Amsterdam for a number of years."

Emma remained impassive. She had the air of a woman who was used to disappointments. Broken relationships with her husband and lover, the death of patients she nursed and the loss of her daughter were a part of her life. She expected the worst and was rarely wrong. "And?" she said.

Mandy really felt for this woman and could hardly bring herself to tell her that her daughter had died in a tiny squalid flat in Amsterdam. She had been laying undiscovered for nearly a week and no one had noticed or cared, just another dead junkie.

"She is not alive. I am so sorry. The Dutch Police will deal with the details but she was discovered earlier today, She had overdosed. I am so sorry .."

"I understand," said Emma interrupted Mandy. "Thank you for letting me know. I should like if you left now."

Chapter 33

Mandy had just come off the phone from listening to Superintendent Taylor. She had been left in no doubt that her lack of progress was not going unnoticed. She sat at her desk staring at the phone. She knew he was right. The investigation into the baby's death had completely stalled and with Millicent's dead there was now little hope of uncovering the circumstances of the murder.

Adrian Bennet's murder, apart from the sighting of a Volkswagen car by a neighbour at the scene was not yielding any further clues. John Reynolds' murder scene had been completely trashed of any forensic evidence by the storm on the night of his murder. The Greek police seemed to be quite happy to write off Francis Dowally's death as accidental. Her only remaining suspects Peter Ward and Rod Hardy were alibiing each other on the night of Reynolds' murder.

She had Merryweather, Potts and Siskin going over the phone records of everyone in detail. That was proving a monumental task. Only Bennet had but one phone. Ward, Reynold and Hardy had multiple phones associated with their business. There was no realistic way of tracking calls made to the switchboards and then subsequently transferred to them.

In truth establishing communication between the members of Lost in Time around the time of the discovery of the Millicent's baby proved very little. Even if she could prove that Francis Donally had phoned one of them from Crete and they had subsequently communicated with each other it did not place them at the scene of her death. The same applied to Bennet's and Reynold's murders. It would not place anyone at the murder scenes.

Merryweather, Potts and Siskin had spent hundreds of man hours trying to get a fix on Ward's and Hardy's mobile phones. They had not been successful. Nether's phone could be placed in the vicinity of Bennet's or Reynold's murder. Of course it did not mean they had not committed the murders it merely meant that their phones were not present.

The car satellite navigation systems, of the suspects were another means, they considered to track their movements. She did not have enough evidence to size their vehicles. In any event, only Hardy's car was fitted with a factory Sat Nav that recorded the data. Ward's Volkswagen was too old to have factory fitted Sat Nav.

Mandy knew she needed to develop further lines of enquiries. She had three unsolved murders, two suspects and no evidence. She flicked through the reports strewn across her desks. Her team had gone door to door, no one had seen anything around the time Reynolds had been murdered. The only sighting was the car at Bennet's and that could just be a neighbour confusing the time or day his nurse called.

They had trolled through hours of CCTV footage. They were hoping to get footage of a suspect's car at one of the crime scenes. The Automatic Number Plate Recognition system had picked up Hardy's movements on the motorways and major roads but not near Normans Bay or Bennett's cottage. Tracks and minor roads were just not covered.

A young girl had been groomed by Ward, Hardy, Reynold's and Bennet. Donally had also played her part standing by or even taking advantage of her to satisfy her sexual needs. . Despite denials they had sexually used a school girl for their own satisfaction, supplied her with drink and drugs and pimped her to others as a source of income. Mandy knew that she had to get justice for Millicent and her baby.

How had her baby come to be killed and entombed, in a wall in a flat in Eastbourne? Had Millicent played a part in the murder of her own child? Had they all decided to get rid of the problem or had just one person decided the course of action? Francis Donally was clearly about to talk and had been silenced. Mandy suspected that seeing the news of the baby's discovery, Millicent had been overcome by guilt and deliberately overdosed. There was no way to know now.

Sam's theory that Bennet and Reynolds had been murder to silence them needed further examination. She asked herself why now? Anyone of them could have come forward in the last seven years or at the time of the baby's death. Would the finding of the body be enough to prompt a change of heart? For Donally it had been but for the others? She thought not.

If she assumed that none of the male members had any motivation to confess to child grooming, paedophilia or infanticide then what was the motive behind Reynolds and Bennet's murders. They were not about to spill the beans, so why kill them?

What had she missed? She had an uneasy feeling over the past few days. It was a niggling thought at the back of her mind. What was it? She had seen something. She had seen it twice now. Something pulled at her thoughts. Where and what had she seen?

She started retracing her her steps over the last few days, the crime scene at Bennet's, Normans Bay, Reynold's body, her interviews with Ward and Hardy. It was tantalising close. Her trip to Dartford, Emma Nooks, Gatwick and Amsterdam, They whirled around her head.

"Sam," she suddenly shouted out, attracting the whole teams attention. She began scrabbling through the files on her desk.

"What is it?" said Sam slightly breathless despite only having jogged fifteen yards across the incident room to her office.

"Here," she said. "Here staring me in the face. I must be blind. Even you pointed it out to me. Track this." She handed him the file.

Chapter 34

Mandy knew that time was not on her side as she sat waiting for Superintendent Taylor to become free. Brighton Nick was bustling with activity. She had arrived early and walked into the change over of the day shift. People were trying to get off home and hand off their investigations. Taylor was in a briefing with the other senior officers. It had obviously been a hectic shift as she was kept waiting for nearly an hour. Eventually she was summoned.

"Well?" said Taylor.

"Good Morning, Sir," said Mandy.

"Yes, yes, what do you want? I am busy here."

"I want a warrant to search a number of premises." She pushed the applications across the table. He started to read. It did not take long.

"Well you won't get a magistrate to grant you one based on this. You don't have anything that remotely smacks of evidence. It is just a theory."

Mandy knew he was right. She also knew that with the right support form a senior officer, such as Taylor and a friendly magistrate it was possible she could get what she wanted. "Could you not obtain them? I mean your request would carry some weight."

"It wouldn't for long if I randomly applied for warrants to search half the population of East Sussex." he replied.

"I know I am right.."

"You can know all you want. When you have a single piece of solid evidence, come back and you'll get your warrant. Now I am busy."

She had plenty of time on the drive to Eastbourne to reflect on matters. She knew that Taylor was right. She was sure that she knew who had committed murder but she had no real proof that would hold up in Court. The Crown Prosecution Service would not take a case to trial that did not have a reasonable chance of resulting in a conviction.

She pulled up, parked and made her way into Eastbourne Police Station. The team were already assembled awaiting her arrival. She had hoped to be in a position to send them out and make the searches. She did not delay in informing them of the outcome of her meeting with Taylor. "No go," she said.

Merryweather spoke. "There is something that might cheer you up. It is just in. I sent the Greek police pictures of the our suspects. They tracked the Taverna where Donally and a male had lunch, as you know. It was the last sighting of her. The owner of the restaurant was not one hundred per cent but he picked out one."

Mandy looked at the photograph. "That doesn't get us much further."

"Agreed," said Potts. "Siskin and I have been working around the clock on phone records. It was a nightmare, what with office phones and the suspects mobiles. We have done a chart."

Siskin placed it in front of Mandy. She and Sam began to study it as Potts talked. "Look you can see the activity suddenly start when the baby's discovery is made public knowledge by the media. They have clearly lied in their statements. They were all in touch with each other and the discovery of the body prompted the flurry of phone calls. They were all getting their stories straight before we turned up asking questions."

"Or plotting murder to cover it up," said Potts.

Sam spoke."We can't know what was said. All it proves is that they got in touch with one another. They will argue that was a perfectly normal thing to do. After all the body of a baby had turned up in a flat they used to share. It helps but it doesn't get the warrants."

"What do we have so far," said Mandy. "We have motive. Lives have moved on and no one wants to be incarcerated for the death of Millicent's baby. So we have initially a whole load of suspects that have been drastically reduced by more murders and possible suicide ."

She paused and thought for a moment. "We have some evidence. The car spotted by a neighbour at Bennett's, the English man having lunch with Donally, Ward and Hardy in Eastbourne when Reynolds is murdered and now phone evidence linking the parties. We also have them all lying on record about their contact with Millicent, her supposed death and their involvement in the fatal car crash that killed Christine Darmer."

"We need to get Ward and Hardy in and apply pressure," said Sam.

"We will only have the one shot," said Mandy. "I can't see them admitting to anything without more evidence. We have to make them break ranks. Turn on each other. They just need to keep stum, lawyer up and they will walk out of here."

"There is one last thing. I can't see how it helps but I have checked with DVLA as to cars registered to them all. I an not sure but what good it is but here's the list," said Merryweather.

Mandy looked at it. She looked up smiling. "I think, my merry band of Policeman that we have the key."

She took a pen and forms. "I am authoring the arrest of the following on suspicion of murder. Once they are arrested send in search teams."

Mandy and Sam were left alone as Potts, Siskin and Merryweather teamed up with uniformed officers and headed off to make the arrests. "You are really putting it on the line. We don't have sufficient evidence to charge, do we? "

"That's a matter of opinion. The Courts can test the evidence later. As it stands now that they are under arrest, we can search."

"But you are charging everyone with murder?"

"There's a good reason for that," said Mandy.

Chapter 35

Sam and Mandy sat in her office waiting. The suspects had been seized and were being held in custody. Searches of their homes and cars had been carried out. Their cell phones had been taken when they arrived at the Police Station. Their phones along with their car satellite navigation systems were being analysed to trace their movements.

Sam broke the silence. "You do realise that if the searches and data analysis turn up nothing then we had affectively blown any chance in the case?"

"Of course I do," said Mandy and the tension sounded in her reply. " There is only one possible solution and so it has to be correct but the evidence is another matter."

"Well it beats me. We can't place either Ward or Hardy at the scene of Bennet's or Reynolds murders. Even if their phones or cars put them in the vicinity that would be highly circumstantial. We would need to place the killer at the scene, at the time of death preferable with the weapon or some forensic evidence. The best you can hope for is a GPS track of their movements from their electronic devices."

"It would be a start at least," she said.

"The murder of Francis Donally seems totally out of reach. We have a tentative ID but that only proves that she had lunch with someone. That's a far cry form placing him at the murder scene and committing the deed."

Mandy nodded her head. "You are right. There seems little chance of tying Ward and Hardy to the death of Donally or implicating Bennet and Reynolds. Even if we wanted to get involved in the case of Francis Donally there is no way the Greek Police would hand over the investigation. To be honest neither would we. What self respecting Police Force wants to admit it is not up to carrying out its own investigations. There is still one murder that you seem to be missing out here."

"Baby Nook, there is even less hope of proving who did that, surely?"

"I am sorry you think that but that is exactly what I am going to prove."

"I don't see how? We have nothing, absolute zero in evidence to charge anyone. Even the Mother is dead. She overdosed on heroine in Amsterdam and she was the most likely suspect," said Sam.

"You are sometimes a little black and white in your thinking. I look at Millicent and I do not see a murderer. I see a victim. A young girl that is vulnerable. She is unhappy at home. She is befriended by some wanna be pop stars. She is groomed. She is supplied with drugs and alcohol. She is used. She is pimped. She is a child and she is pregnant."

"Okay but .."

"It is anything but okay however you look at it. We have a group of paedophiles and I am sure Francis Donally even took advantage of her, who moved on with their lives. The baby was conveniently disposed of and Millicent abandoned, while Lost in Time was on tour in the Netherlands.

"I understand but I still not see where it gets us?"

"You need to turn the triangle and view it from a different point of view. Millicent and her baby were the victims. I am convinced that she lived with her guilt. It slowly ate at her. She was a child when these men and women groomed her. She was a child when she became pregnant. She was a child when her baby was born. She didn't kill that baby they did."

"She lost her childhood and her self esteem. She was a prostitute addicted and with no sense of self worth. I believe that she saw that the body had finally been found and that was the tipping point. She decided that was enough. The floods gates broke. She committed suicide and deliberately overdosed on heroine."

"You can't know that. There was no note. In ninety percent of suicides there is some sort of note," said Sam.

"Um, I am not sure about you statistics but I agree that there is mostly a suicide note. And I don't think Millicent was any different. I am sure there was a note." said Mandy.

"But there was no note."

"There was. We just haven't found it yet," said Mandy.

The conversation was brought to an end by the appearance of Siskin and Potts. They knocked and entered the office. "The Sat Nav results are in," said Potts and passed the paperwork to Mandy.

"The phones results are in as well," said Siskin and followed suit with the paperwork.

"You take the Sat Navs and I'll do the mobile phones," said Mandy to Sam as the two DCs left the office.

Sam began to go through the suspects car movements comparing them against the the murders of Bennet and Reynolds. Mandy did the same for the suspects mobile phones. It was a slow process. They sat in silence for the next two hours while the suspects waited in their cells.

Sam finally looked up and rubbed his eyes. "Nothing I have nothing. They were nowhere near the crime scene or at least their cars weren't. Now what?"

Mandy did not respond but concentrated on the phones. Sam just looked out of her window at the darken skies as the rain clouds gathered yet again for another downpour. He knew that they could only hold their prisoners for twenty four hours and then they would have to charge them or let them go. Much as he trusted Mandy he felt that this time she had overreached herself. They had their chance and now they would walk free. Realistically there would be no second bite of the cherry. Once let go there was no bringing them in again, without significant further evidence.

He watched as she searched the phone data. She made notes as she went. Then she eventual lent back in her chair and smiled. "What?" he said.

"We are ready to interview our first candidate. Get Emma Nook to the interview room and I will meet you there."

Chapter 36

"I don't understand why I am here?" Emma Nook's voice was unsteady as she spoke. A uniformed officer stood at the door to the interview room, while Mandy and Sam sat on one side of the table with Emma opposite. The voice recorder was on and CCTV monitored the proceedings.

"You have been informed of your right to remain silent and the your right to have a lawyer present," said Sam.

Emma nodded. "I don't want a lawyer," she said. She did not protest her arrest, nor need she seem to be surprised. Her body reflected her mood of resignation, even of indifference.

Mandy began to speak. "I want to talk to you about the murder of Adrian Bennet."

Emma remained silent almost distracted.

"You did not ask me who Adrian Bennet was? I wonder why that is? How is it possible you knew the name Mrs Nook?"

"I have nothing to say," came the reply.

"I also want to talk about the murder of John Reynolds?"

"I have nothing to say," came the reply. It was clear that Emma was

169

not going to engage.

"Again I note that you clearly know the name of the victim. Can I ask how you know him?" Emma remained quiet.

Mandy took a slow intake of breath before she continued. "I am going to take you through how I arrived at this point. I think once you see your position. I think you may want to help."

"Mr Bennet was murdered by someone driving a Volkswagen. A neighbour spotted what he assumed was his nurse's car at the time of the murder. It could not have been her car. She had called much earlier in the day."

"When Sam and I visited you, on each occasion we found it difficult to park. It did not register at the time but there was always a Volkswagen parked in the vicinity. It was not parked outside your house. Parking space is at a premium in your road as there are no garages for the houses. You park where you can, as close as you can. You were of course not a suspect at the time merely the mother of a lost girl."

"I began to suspect all was not as it seemed when we interview you. Sam even picked up on you lack of emotion at being told you daughter had been the victim of mistaken identity. On being told that your daughter had not been killed years earlier in a car crash you hardly reacted. At the time we put it down to shock. People do after all have different reactions."

"You lack of emotional engagement however became even more surprising, when I informed you that your daughter had been found dead in Amsterdam. Any mother hearing of the death of their child, her only child would surely exhibit some form of grief."

Emma bowed her head and still said nothing.

"Not only in a short space of time had you heard that you daughter was alive and then overdosed on heroine but you also found out that her baby, your grandchild had been murdered. Yet you still exhibited neither grief nor asked about the murder of a baby. Why was that, Emma? Why did you not ask what we were doing to catch the murderer?"

"I couldn't take it all in. It was just overwhelming," came the reply.

"I don't think so," said Mandy. "At the time we had no reason to suspect you of being involved in Bennet's murder. After all, you did not, could not, have known the names of the suspects in the murder of your granddaughter. If you had heard nothing from Millicent, since the day she went missing you had no way of knowing anything of her life thereafter. You could not have know she was living in the flat only miles from you. You could not have known that she had been groomed by Peter Ward and was being used by Bennet, Hardy and Reynolds. That she had been pimped by them. That they had introduced her to hard drugs. How could you have know what they had done to your daughter."

There was silence. Mandy looked at Emma and saw hate in her eyes.

"You did knew though, didn't you? I watched as I mentioned the names of your daughters abusers, Hardy, Ward, Reynolds and Bennet. You already knew their names. You also knew they were responsible for the death of Millicent's baby. Didn't you? You knew long before DS Shaw and I turned up at your house."

"You missed that bitch Donally out. She was as bad as the rest of then. She used her. She was no different. They are all scum. They should all rot in hell, " Emma spoke, her venom and hate was evident.

Mandy continued pushing for more. "Putting aside how you knew what had happened to Millicent and her baby, I focussed on you as a suspect. You had the strongest motive for wanting these people dead."

"The question that faced me was the how? How does a middle aged, woman , a nurse go about killing them? You started closest to home, with Bennet. Even though I suspected that you drove to his house and stabbed him, at first I could not fathom how you knew where to find him. It was of course easy for you. You are a nurse are you not?"

Emma nodded. She had calmed herself.

"You are a senior nurse. You have access to patients records, their doctors records and above all their addresses. It was easy to find Bennet, once you knew the name. In fact a quick internet search of the band, Lost in Time and its members would have given you enough data to find them. I have had a quick look. Their biogs are on line, date of birth, education and early career are all there a few clicks of the mouse away. That coupled with access to NHS medical records gave you everything you needed, addresses, even contact details, phone and email."

"So you knew who and where they were. The only thing I have to do is place you at the scene of the murders. We took your cell phone when you came into custody. This Emma, is a list of your mobile calls and an analysis of your movements. You had your phone map setting enabled. We can see exactly where you have been and when."

Emma glanced at the sheets of paper Mandy presented to her. "It places you at the scene, at the time of Adrian Bennet's murder. You drove to his house. You were in your nurses uniform. The witness was right about the car, the time and even thinking it was a nurse. In any event, Bennet would have no suspicions when you arrived. You only then had to take a knife from the kitchen and finish what you had set out to do."

"He deserved to die for what he had done," said Emma. The vitriol in her voice apparent.

"Your phone shows that you rang John Reynolds. What I am uncertain of is how you persuaded him to meet you at Normans Bay? Anyway now that we have you phone we can also see from his phone records that you spoke on the day of his murder. Your phone again puts you at the location at the time of his death."

"I told him I was a friend of Millicent's and I had a letter signed by her, telling me how the death of her baby came about. I said I wanted twenty thousand pounds for it. If he didn't pay up I told him I would take it to you."

"And then you stabbed him in the car park?" said Sam.

"It was easy. He really thought everyone was like him, money grasping morally corrupt. I don't think he even realised at first that I had stabbed him and that he was dying. It was easy after killing Bennet."

"You know I am going to charge you with the murder of John Reynolds and Adrian Bennet, don't you?" said Mandy.

"I don't really care. My life ended when Millicent killed herself in Amsterdam. It was all I could do to make amends for all I had done wrong. I let her down, She should never have ended up where she did. I am as guilty as those bastards, that band, their scumbag manager. She was just a child. I was too adsorbed in my new boyfriend, rebuilding my life, selfish but they took advantage of her. They used her. They took what they wanted and didn't care about that damage, the devastation or even the death of a baby. My only regret is that I couldn't finish what I had started. A few more days and I would have done the same to Ward and Hardy."

"I know. You have already phoned both of them. The calls are in the phone record in front of you. I am guessing that you used the same tactic as you did on Reynolds. Asking for money for a so called letter incriminating them, to lure them to their deaths?"

"Yes," she said. Her emotion was one of disappointment at not finishing the job.

"There is only one last question," said Mandy. "That is, how did you know about Donally, Hardy, Bennet, Ward and Reynolds?"

"You are so clever, you seem to know everything else why don't you tell me?" Emma said.

"There is only one explanation. Millicent, drug addicted and surviving by prostitution saw the news. She saw that her dead baby's body had been found, discarded like a piece of rubbish. Shoved in a hole in a wall and plastered over. She was no longer a child. She now realised that she had been groomed, sexually abused, pimped and discarded. To be reminded of that and to have to face that you were a party to the murder of your own newborn baby must have been unbearable. Guilt, shame, self loathing and disgust must have consumed her mind. She determined to find peace. She had enough. She saw her own death as a way out or even contrition. She just could not go on any more."

Tears were running down Emma's face now. "I should have been there." she sobbed.

"Millicent wanted to do one last thing. She wanted you to know what had happened. She wanted you to know that she did not blame you. She wanted the comfort before she ended it, to know that perhaps in the whole World that there might be at least one person that would remember her. One person that might just care a tiny little bit about her."

"She had no email address, for you. Your phone number had changed. The only way of contacting you was by letter. So before she died she did write a letter to you. We know she had to have made contact. There is no other way you could know of Hardy and the others in Lost in Time."

"She wrote to me. She told me everything. When you arrived to tell me that she might still be alive, I already knew she had killed herself. I did not know where she was. There was nothing I could do. I let her down yet again. She died alone. So I did the only thing I could I set about making them suffer, the way they had made her suffer. I don't care about me. I just want that scum dead. My only regret is that you caught me before I managed to finish ."

"I am charging you with the murders of Adrian Bennet and John Reynolds but I don't have enough evidence to charge Ward or Hardy," said Mandy.

Emma Nook looked at Mandy. "Get the bastards for me," she said. She reached in her handbag and gave Mandy the letter.

Chapter 37

Dear Mum,

I know this must come as a big shock but it is me Millicent. I know that you have thought me dead all these years but it I am not. Please, please try and understand I did what I did because I thought it for the best. I will tell you what happened and I hope you can forgive me. If you can't it doesn't really matter as I cannot forgive myself.

When Dad left I felt that it was my fault. I know that makes no sense but it did to me then. He wrote to me. I don't know if you knew that but he wrote one letter. It was an angry letter. It just said that he wasn't my Dad. He said he didn't know who my Dad was and he could never know. He said that he couldn't trust you and that you had cheated on him with loads of men and that's why.

Of course he never contacted us again. He was there one minute and then he wasn't, my Dad and then he was gone, gone from my life. I am not sure what age I was, twelve, thirteen when he went. I know I had just changed school. I never fitted there. I was bullied everyday. They said all sorts of things about you. I was so lonely.

Then out of nowhere Tom moved in. It was like you just swapped him for Dad. I knew he hated me. I was in the way. I wasn't his kid and he didn't want me around. You always took his part. I was alone. You had pushed Dad out and he didn't want to see me any more. You moved

Tom in and I was in your way, mucking up your like, an inconvenience.

Anyway that's how I felt as a teenager. Now I know that life is not so black and white but that's how I felt then. I was on my own. I felt I needed punishing. There had to be a reason why you both didn't want me. Cutting myself helped. It started small but the self harming got worse and worse. The blood and cuts were a release. I felt better. The deeper I cut the better it felt. I hated myself and I hated my life.

You never picked up on the cutting. I was careful to do it where it wasn't easily seen, on my thighs or chest. It was my secret. It made me feel better. I would stand in front of the mirror and watch the cuts bleeding. It was as though I deserved it and it felt right.

Things just got worse with you and Tom. I hated him more and more and I hated you for always taking his side. I just hated everything, school, home, Tom, you but mostly myself. I dreaded waking up and going to school, I hated the kids and the teachers. I would pretend to go to school and wait for you to leave then change out of my uniform. I would just spend the day hanging out.

I stared nicking stuff from the shops in the town centre, crisps , chocolate and fizz. I couldn't always get back in the house to change my clothes because you worked shifts at the hospital. When you were off during the day I couldn't get back in to change. That's when I started stealing clothes

I soon met people like me. We hung out in the parks or on the beach. We would nick booze or sell stuff we had stolen to buy booze. We would get drunk or get high. You didn't seem to notice. You were to wrapped up with Tom. I would get back off my face but it was like I didn't exist as long as I kept out of your way.

When I first met Peter Ward I was completely out of it. He was a lot older but he was nice to me. He bought me stuff, food, booze and the odd present. It was so flattering. I was totally fixated on him. He told me I was special and that he loved me. It felt to me that for once I mattered and I was not just a burden. He told me that he understood me and that I should trust him.

He started having sex with me. Of course now I see he groomed me. At the time I did not see that. I just that he was wonderful and loved me. At last I had someone who wanted me for being me. It did not take long before he had me sleeping with other men. Peter told me that if we were to be together we needed money. I felt I was doing it so we could be together.

He took me to the flat he shared with John Reynolds, Adrian Bennet and woman called Francis Donally. It was a party house and it was not long before I had moved on from weed to crack cocaine and then smoking heroine. They were all doing it. Peter told me that they shared everything.

It did not take me long to find out what he meant by that. They all took it in turns to have sex with Francis and me. She was older and she liked girls as well as men. They used to get us to perform for them. We were used. I see that now. They would bring men in and they would pay. It kept us in food and most importantly drugs. They would play music and had a manger, Rod Hardy. He paid the rent and got them gigs. Francis and I always had to be nice to Rod.

It was becoming impossible at home. I was out of it most of the time. One day I just never bothered to come back. I was a wreck I didn't know where I was. It wasn't even a conscious decision. Lost in Time became my new family so I just moved in.

I went where they went. They would get in their van or at least a van Rod lent them and drive up and down the country playing. It was a

178

blur, drugs, drink music and sex with anyone that paid. Then we played a gig somewhere, Birmingham or Coventry? I don't really remember. Peter had managed to get a young girl off her face. I didn't know her name at the time. Later I found out she was called Christine Darmer.

The four of us, me, Peter, John and Christine left the pub where Lost in Time had performed. We got something to eat, chips or a kebab. I don't remember. We smoked some crack. I don't know how it happened but we ended up in a car. I think John or Peter nicked it. John was driving, I was in the front. Peter and Christine were in the back. I remember her getting naked. John was taking Christine's clothes off.

I can't remember the details but the car crashed and we ended up in a field. It caught fire and we we just staggering around. We didn't even notice that Christine was still in the car. I don't know how. I suppose some one must have phoned but we got back to the road and the van turned up. Rod was driving and we drove back to Eastbourne.

Everyone expected the police to turn up but they didn't. We watched the news. There was a short bit about a girl's body being found. Somehow they named her as me. I have no idea how they got us mixed up. We celebrated getting away with it, more drink and drugs. I know it was wrong but at the time I thought you wouldn't care if I was alive or dead. So I let it be.

The party went on. Lost in Time grew more popular. They started to get noticed. I was doing more and more drugs. The whole thing is hazy and I can't remember most of it. I thought I had a dream. A nightmare would be a better description.

I couldn't tell what was real or what were was not, I was so junked up. We were doing anything we could get our hands. I remember feeling terrible pains. I know I was laying naked on a mattress at the flat. John was having a really bad acid trip. We had all done LSD and God knows

179

what else. It was crazy, out of control.

I remember Francis screaming. I remember pain but very little else. I was so drugged up. Now I know I had a baby but then I didn't know what was happening. I didn't even know I was pregnant. My belly was a bit bigger but I didn't really show. Until a few days ago I never really knew what had happened. I thought it had been a bad trip.

Peter and Adrian were really tripped out. Screaming about the devil. I thought it was all in my head. I saw a baby. They seemed to be screaming at it. It was drug fuelled madness. There was some sort of fight. Francis was screaming. Adrian seemed to be fighting with Peter. A baby was crying. Then there was silence, the baby stopped crying. Peter was holding the limp body.

I was out of it for days when I sort of came out of it there was nothing. I staggered to the bathroom and Rod was doing some repairs to the wall. I had a piss. I was sore and bleeding. I assumed that I had been used while I was unconscious. It was not the first time I had woken up with torn genitals. I just assumed I had had sex with a few men. It was the norm.

No one said anything and until two days ago I did not know that what had happened was real. It had seemed so real but I couldn't decide if it had been a drug induced hallucination. I spoke to Rod about it at the time He told me I had just dreamed it and not to be stupid.

Rod got me a passport and they went on tour on the Continent. I don't know if it was planed but when we got to the Netherlands Rod introduced me to a Romanian who called himself Akash. I went with him. Rod said I was to pick up some dope and bring it back for the band.

Akash took me to an old building. As soon as I was inside he threw me in a room with three other girls. I started to argue and tried to leave.

He just beat me. He said he had paid Rod for me and I had better do as I was told. I was kept a prisoner along with the other trafficked girls. Akash and two other Romanians pimped us. We got nothing and they kept all the money.

There was one difference between me and the other girls. They were illegal and their captures were controlling them by threaten their families back home. They had been trafficked into thinking they were going into paid work. The traffickers said they owed money and they had to work the debt off.

I waited and eventually got away from them. I don't know what happened to them. I didn't care. I just found myself homeless and penniless in Amsterdam. I did what I had to, to get by. I work for myself. I don't have a pimp.

I know you must find all of this shocking but I needed to tell some one. I write because I saw on the news that a baby had been found walled up in a flat in Eastbourne, my baby, your grandchild. I know now that it was not dream, an hallucination. It happened. I had a baby. Peter and Adrian murdered my baby and the rest of them went along with it and got rid of me as soon as they could.

I hate them all. They used me and discarded me. I feel so tired. I feel so much hate, hate for them and hate for myself. I am going to end it all. By the time you receive this letter I will be dead.

I just wanted you to know what happened to me. I guess you probably don't care and have your own life. I will never understand why you never loved me. I didn't ask to be on this Planet.

Millicent.

Chapter 38

"Well, one down two to go," said Mandy. She and Sam were making their way along the corridor to interview Rod Hardy. He was waiting for them with his solicitor. Siskin and Merryweather had taken Emma Nook to the front desk, where the custody sergeant was booking her in for murder.

The solicitor's name was Baker and after the formalities had been completed, he decided to speak first "I have advised my client to answer no comment to all you questions. He has however prepared a statement which he wishes to read."

"I see. I think that would be just fine," said Mandy. "Off you go then."

"I was the manager of a group called Lost in Time. Between 2011 and 2016 I rented a flat in Eastbourne from a Mr Christos Koumi. I did not reside at the residence. I allowed the following to live there, John Reynolds, Adrian Bennet, Peter Ward and Francis Donally all of whom were members of the band, Lost In Time. I rarely attended the premises. I was aware that they would have friends to stay occasionally. I cannot recall the names of any of those guests except for a young lady, whom I knew as Millie. I believe she must have been a girlfriend of one of the band members as, I think I saw her there on more that one occasion.

I have no knowledge of the death of and subsequently interment of the body of a baby at the premises. As I previously stated I rarely attend the flat and had little knowledge of the occupants outside of our professional relationship. I deny any knowledge of any and all illegal activity, which any one or all of the residents may or may not have been involved."

"That seems to clear that up then," said Sam sarcastically, interrupting Hardy.

"Sadly and I mean from your client's point of view that account does not correspond with the facts in our possession, " said Mandy.

"You seem to be confusing facts with conjecture and superstitious, DCI Pile," replied Baker. ""As we understand it the only other person who can shed light on the events that occurred during this period is Mr Ward. I understand from my client that he will also be unable to add very little to what my client recalls."

"I was not referring to Mr Ward. I realise that you client and Mr Ward have had ample time to get their stories straight.

Baker began to bluster. "Hold on there, let the DCI finish and then you can do the righteous indignation bit," said Sam.

"As I was saying Mr Ward has not yet been interviewed under caution. I hope you note that your client is being given the chance to give his account of events first. A point you may wish to reflect on. So before I continue, I say again is there anything you wish to add to your prepared statement?"

"No comment," came the reply.

"As you like. I have hear a written statement from Millicent Nook. She had been located by the Dutch Police living in Amsterdam. So I asked again would you like to revise your position or would you, Mr Baker like to revise your advice to your client. I should say this document does not align with what Mr Hardy has just read out." She held the letter up briefly.

"May I see that?" said Baker.

"Not at this stage. I would like to pose a number of questions to Mr Hardy and then the statement will be entered into evidence at the discovery phase. "I can further add we are in the process of having Millicent returned to the UK."

"May I have a minute alone with my client," said Baker..

"Of course, interview suspended." The tape was switched off along with the CCTV. She and Sam left Hardy and his solicitor to discuss matters in private.

Standing in the corridor, Sam spoke first. "What was that about flying Millicent back to give evidence, she's dead."

"I didn't say that did I? I said she was being returned to the UK and she is. Well at least her body is, to be buried here. I am guessing that Hardy doesn't know she is dead."

"But you have the letter that implicates him anyway."

"I am not sure how that stacks up in court. It is not a sworn affidavit. It will carry some weight as it was written in anticipation of her suicide but it cannot be tested in Court obviously as she is dead. It would be better if Hardy admits to his part under caution with his solicitor present. Don't you think?" said Mandy.

They were interrupted by a knock on the interview room door from the inside. It was the signal or them to resume the interview. The tapes and cameras were turned back on and they all resumed their places.

"In the light of what you have told us my client it appears to have had his memory jogged and feels he may be in a position to further your inquiries," said Baker.

"That's nice," said Sam.

"Let's start with the night Lost in Time played at the Lady Godiva?"

Rod Hardy took a moment to gather his thoughts. "We all drove up in the Van. I drove. I had to drive because the chances of any of the rest of them being sober or drug free was one in a million. They played the gig and we loaded the gear back onto the van. I was anxious to get back but Peter and John were nowhere about."

"Did Millicent travel with you to the gig?"

"Yes, she was more or less there all the time. Peter seemed to have her under his spell. Anyway we sat around waiting for them to appear. I am not sure what the exact time was but I got a call from them. They said they were stuck and needed a lift. I got the rest of them into the van. We found the three of them down some deserted road In the middle of nowhere."

"Did you see the burning car?"

" I saw what appeared to be a fire about a mile away. It was only after it was on the news that I realised what it was. They had walked some distance from the crash."

"Tell me about Millicent's baby," said Mandy.

"I had nothing to do with that."

"I remind you I have Millicent's testimony in front of me."

"I had nothing to do with her death. I had no idea she was pregnant, there were no visible signs that I picked up on. I have to say I paid her little attention. She was just there in the background and usually out of it on drugs as far as I remember. When I turned up at the flat all hell had broken out. Millicent was lying in the corner. She was so drugged up and drunk she didn't even realise what had happened. There was a dead baby, Peter and Adrian were ranting about demons, devils and God know what."

"Who decided to hide the body?"

"I suppose I did. It was stupid, a moment of madness, I had nothing to do with the murder though. She was dead when I got there."

"You sold Millicent to people traffickers in the Netherlands though," interrupted Sam.

"My client denies that," said Baker.

"What about the murder of Francis Donally, has you client anything to say about that?" said Mandy.

"No comment." said Hardy.

"We have and an application from the Greek police in connection with the matter. Your photograph has been identified by a Taverna owner. You had lunch in Crete with Francis on the day of her death."

"No comment,"

"I am charging you as an accessory after the fact to the murder of Millicent's baby and obstructing the police."

Chapter 39

It was clear that Rod hardy and Peter Ward had decided on their strategy prior to their arrest. Sam and Mandy were confronted with the same scenario they had previously encountered from Hardy, as they sat down to interview Peter Ward. The solicitor was different. A man called Drew.

"I have advised my client to make no comment but he wishes to read a prepared statement," said Drew. Mandy and Sam sat quietly while Ward denied any knowledge of Millicent apart from her occasional attendance at the flat or any knowledge of the existence of a baby.

"That was very interesting," said Sam.

"Except it was completely untrue," said Mandy. "I would suggest that you speak to your client and advise him to cooperate. I assure you we can prove his statement to be false."

There was a moment's silence before Drew replied. "My client sticks by his statement."

"As you like but don't say we didn't warn you," said Sam.

"It may be of interest to you to know that we have located Millicent Nook. She is in the Netherlands but you already know that because that is where you and Mr Hardy abandoned her in the care of some people traffickers." Concern began to appear on Ward's face as she spoke.

Mandy continued. "I should like to examine you statement a little closer. You say that you had little contact with her, that she was an occasional visitor at the flat and stopped there occasionally. Now would it surprise you that Millicent says you were her boyfriend, had regular sex with her and encouraged her to have sex with others for money ?"

Ward looked at his solicitor for guidance. There was none forthcoming. He remained taciturn.

"Okay, still nothing to say I see. You were of course aware that Millicent was fourteen years old, a child. Would it be fair to say that you took advantage of a vulnerable child and deliberately set out to groom her?"

"No comment," he said.

"I am astonished that you do not wish to deny the allegation given the serious nature of the offence. I understand that you have applied for a top job in the social care sector. Given that it would bring you into even closer contact with children than even your current post are you sure that you still wish to make no comment in the matter?"

Ward was becoming increasing agitated and looking at his solicitor. Drew was clearly uncomfortable at the turn of events. He was also displaying thinly veiled distaste for his client but urged his client to remain silent.

"I should like to turn to the events that led to the death of Christine Darmer. You were a member of the group Lost in Time and playing at a venue in Coventry called the Lady Godiva."

"Before you bother to no comment, you should bear in mind we have the poster showing that you were playing there that night," Sam

188

interrupted.

"We know that you and John Reynolds stole a car. The vehicle subsequently crashed. Mr Hardy confirms that he drove to the scene of the crash in the groups van and picked you, Reynolds and Millicent up then drove back to Eastbourne. We will be adding a further charge of causing death by dangerous driving, by the way"

Ward was clearly beginning to panic. "I wasn't driving, " he blurted out in desperation.

"That's progress. So you admit to being the car and clearly you were a lot closely acquainted with Millicent than your prepared statement would have us believe. Who was driving?"

"John," he replied. Drew shook his head willing his client to stop talking.

"Let's turn to the baby walled up in the flat, shall we? You and your flat mates were on LSD when Millicent gave birth. I am not going into details but you and Adrian Bennet in a state of paranoia brought on by your drug use, freaked out. You killed the baby did you not?"

"it wasn't me. I did nothing it was the others.." he was losing control and becoming frantic.

"So you admit to being there," said Sam.

"You should be aware that Mr Hardy has already confirmed that he helped conceal the body."

"I did not mean it to happen. It didn't even seem real at the time. It seemed a dream, an hallucination I was so out of it. It was only hours later when we came down that it became reality. I phoned Rod and he dealt with it."

"Mr Ward I am charging you with murder, grooming, having sex with a minor and living on the proceeds of immoral earnings," said Mandy.

"I should withdraw your job application as head of child services, if I were you," said Sam.

Chapter 40

Superintendent Taylor arrived unannounced at Eastbourne Police Station. He was wearing a tuxedo and had clearly recently shaved. His face was slightly reddened and he smelt overpoweringly of aftershave. He entered the office, where Mandy and Sam were tidying up lose ends, like a bouncing dog that had just found its ball.

"Well done, well done," he shouted. The excessive bonne humeur was not lost on them.

"You seem very happy," said Sam. It was a condition he often found hard to recognise. As his preferred default setting was curmudgeonly and he had a naturally aversion to any sign of cheerfulness.

"It is a good day, " said Taylor. "A very good day, you have solved four murders. That is a good day in anybody's book."

"Thank you, we are just tidying up the paperwork for the Crown Prosecution Service," said Mandy.

Taylor sat on the desk having first checked it was clean of crumbs not wishing to soil his dinner suit. "Reading through, there are a few areas that I wonder about. For example how did you first come to suspect the mother, Emma Nook?"

"To be fair it wasn't just me, Sam picked up on the vibe as well.

Although at the time and out of context it meant very little. We visited Mrs Nook on several occasions. It was her lack of emotional response that we found puzzling. For example she seemed not at all surprised when we told her her daughter might still be alive. You or I would have, I am sure, been over the moon. She seemed hardly moved," said Mandy.

"When we said that what she thought was her daughter needed to be exhumed, she hardly batted an eyelid," said Sam.

"Again on hearing of her daughter's overdose there was very little emotional response. As I said it meant little at the time."

"So what set you on the right tack?" said Taylor.

"Sam's rubbish parking. Mrs Nook lives on what would be an ex-council estate. There is little provision for parking. The residents have to scrabble for space on the roadside. Cars are parked everywhere, which means you have to drive up and down looking for somewhere. You have to bear in mind that Mrs Nook was not on our radar. She was, as far as we were concerned a nurse and a mother, no more. This is not your stereotypical murderer, far from it. Not being a suspect meant that we had run no background checks on her. "

"We didn't check her finances, car or phone," said Sam.

"We knew that Adrian Bennet's nurse drove a grey Volkswagen . We knew that Ward drove a a Volkswagen of more or less the same colour. The neighbour said that he had seen the nurses car at around the time Bennet was murdered," said Mandy.

"We ruled out his carer being there. Our attention was therefore focused on Ward as the possible perpetrator. He had the best motive if Bennet was having a crises of conscience about the murder of the baby.

Francis Donally had been murdered to silence her in Crete so it would be logical to assume his murder was motivated by the same objective, to silence him."

"The problem was we could not place Ward there. With hindsight there was an obvious reason why we couldn't. He was not there and didn't commit the murder. I was guilty of putting my prejudice before the facts and like many coppers before me ignoring the facts that were inconvenient. Had I ruled out Ward sooner I would surely have seen the obvious and cast the net wider."

"So what changed your thinking?" said Taylor.

"As I said her lack of the correct emotional response rang bells at the the back of my mind but focussed on Ward I didn't listen to them. We drove around looking for parking each time we visited Mrs Nook and each time there was a polo, matching the one seen at Bennet's parked near by. I had a niggle at the back of my mind but couldn't put my finger on it," said Mandy.

"Then it clicked," said Taylor.

"Yes it was so obvious when I thought about it. Of course once we checked with Vehicle licensing I knew we owned the car. The next part was easy but we needed a bit of luck. Bring her in and check her phone. We had that bit of luck. She, like most people had left her maps setting untouched. We could track everywhere she had been. It put her at Bennet's murder scene. The call log showed the call to Reynolds. Her phone put her at the his murder."

"The real bit of good fortune was the letter from her daughter, Millicent. It gave us the detail that we needed to force an admission from Hardy," said Sam.

"The dominoes toppled from there. Ward was left with nowhere to

193

go."

"The case against Hardy for the murder of Francis Donally is very weak," said Taylor.

"There is little we can do on that front," said Mandy. "It is down to the Greek Police. Her murder was committed in their jurisdiction. They have the identification by the Taverna owner. We can prove he left the UK at the time but I agree it would not be enough to secure a conviction," said Mandy.

"I suppose the charges relating to Christine Darmer and the murder of Millicent's baby should put him away here for a good stretch. It will give the Greek's a long time to build their case anyway." said Taylor.

"I must be off." He looked at his watch.

"Something special?" said Sam.

Taylor looked smug as he replied. "I have finally been accepted at the Brownstone Gold Club. It has taken me four years to get it. I am going to the annual diner there. So I am off and to pick up Mrs Taylor."

"You will be mixing with the movers and shakers now Sir. Well done," said Sam somewhat sarcastically.

Taylor left strutting like a peacock. "Pompous arse," said Sam.

"Are you busy tonight?" said Mandy.

"I have a micro waved lasagne lined up in the fridge for dinner. My wife's away for another four days visiting our son, his wife and our granddaughter in Newcastle. It's her fourth birthday tomorrow. Why? Said Sam.

"I think we deserve a good dinner don't you. Forget the lasagne,"

said Mandy.

Their taxi pulled up at the clubhouse and Sam and Mandy got out. It had been a bit of a push but Sam had just had time to get home and put on his diner jacket and Mandy had her little black dress, Jimmy Choo's and Prada Bag. They were just in time. The guests were just about to go in for diner.

There was a look of bewilderment on Superintendent Taylor's face as Mandy and Sam stood alongside him and his wife in the queue waiting to be seated. "What are you doing here?"

"Sorry Sir, we can speak later. Nice to meet you Mrs Taylor. If you excuse us we need to make our way to the top table. My Father is the Captain of Brownstone Gold Club this year."

Sam followed Mandy in. "I suppose it will be better than a micro wave meal. Mind you I hope its is not too fancy. I am not a lover of all this modern fiddling about with food malarkey," he muttered.

"Stop moaning, it will be a fun. I wasn't going to go. My Dad gave me the invite for me and a plus one. The food is brilliant here and you have to admit that the look on Taylor's face was priceless?"

"Plus one, is that a promotion from Detective Sergeant?" said Sam.

Printed in Great Britain
by Amazon